The Book
of
Dog

The Book of Dog

Lark Benobi

∨

Vegetablian Books
Santa Cruz, CA

ISBN-13: 978-0-9996546-1-3
ISBN-10: 0-9996546-1-6

First Vegetablian Press Edition September 2018

Printed in the United States of America

for you

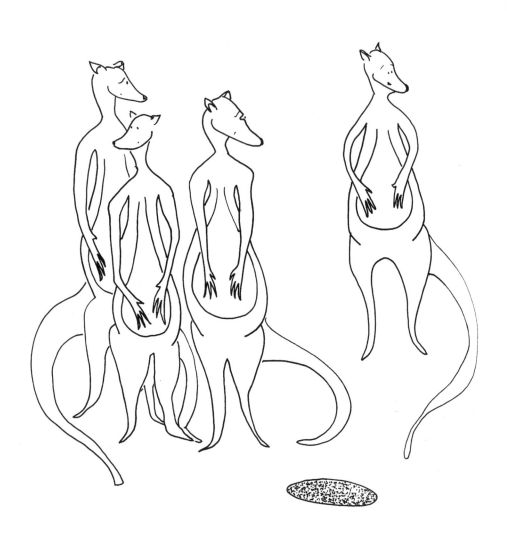

I have no idea who these women are. No idea.

#45

Contents

Book Four: Collapse & Confusion

Book Five: To the Abyss

Book Six: The Land of Nethalem

Book Seven: Beginnings

Prologue

The Ballad at the End of Time

The Ballad at the End of Time

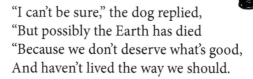

A girl decides to run away.
She leaves her home on Judgment Day.
The land is burnt. The road is wild.
The girl is friendless, and with child.

She finds the Land of Yellow Fog
And there she meets a talking dog.
"What's happening?" the young girl said,
"To make the land so burnt and dead?"

 "I can't be sure," the dog replied,
 "But possibly the Earth has died
 "Because we don't deserve what's good,
 And haven't lived the way we should.

 "Good men automatically rose
 And went to Heaven; and all those
 "With sinful hearts were left behind
 To suffer anguish for all time."

 The girl feels sad. Her feet are weary.
 She dislikes her dog-friend's theory.
 On they flee through yellow fog—
 A pregnant girl, a talking dog—

 And soon they meet a magic bear
 Who gives them food, and combs their hair.
 The bear says, "Well, I don't know why,
 But I must come with you, or die."

The three of them must travel north.
And on their way, they meet the Fourth:
A lonely, injured panther, who
Has lost her friends, and family too.

"We don't have anything to share,"
Says girl, and dog, and magic bear,
"But maybe if we stick together,
Our lives will change, and for the better."

They meet a goat. She greets the Bear.
The goat has feathers in her hair.
"You're very late," the old goat said;
"What hope there was is nearly dead."

"I'm glad you've come at last, but wonder:
Where's our California Condor?"
"Without that Bird, I fear the Beast
Will vanquish us, from first to least."

"Hold on," say bear, and dog, and girl,
"Which Beast is this? Also, which Bird?"
But just then, roaring, from the East
Arrives the Seven-Headed Beast.

"WORSHIP ME!" The foul Beast cries,
And they all quake a bit, inside,
And each of them begins to wonder
If they aren't doomed, without that Condor.

The pregnant girl yells, "Come on, friends!
Let's fight this Beast until the end!"
"While none of us are good, or brave,
Or strong, or best in any way,"

"And though we each are less than least,
Together we can stop this Beast!"
"Stupid girl," the foul Beast cries,
"Worship me, or else, you die."

The panther charges, and begins
To climb the nasty monster's shins
Behind her climbs the mountain goat·
She plans to gore the monster's throat·

And all fight bravely, tooth and claw—
Alas, the Beast defeats them all—
And, looking up through dying eyes,
The dog, before the end, will spy

A far-off condor, coming fast—
She is too late. Her time has passed.
They should be Six. But they are Five.
And soon not one remains alive.

He kills them all. It is their fate
Because the bird arrives too late.

~ Anon.

xiv

The Book
of
Dog

Book One

The Night of the Yellow Puff-Ball Mushroom Cloud

Chapter One
In the Beginning

Woof Say All!

Here is the story of how six unlikely women changed the fate of the world.

In the beginning Mary Mbwembwe was making a cup of chamomile tea. Josefina Guzman was chasing a fox from her yard. Margie Peach was pumping gas into her car. Wanda Lubiejewski was plunging a stopped toilet. Major Eureka Yamanaka was hefting a briefcase into Marine Helicopter Squadron One.

As for Stella King, she was unexpectedly pregnant with the unborn child of the Beast.

It could have happened to anyone. The Beast was a creature of compelling and seductive disguises, and he was known by just as many names, among them: Lix Tetrax, Lucifer, Beelzebub, Chlorpyrifos, Metolachlor, The Anointed Cherub, The Dark Lord, The Pernicious One, The Great Deceiver, and (his personal favorite) The Ruler of the Free World; and he had seduced Stella by disguising himself as a charismatic young Harley rider, and he had wooed her with the false promise of a carefree life spent riding on the back of his Soft Tail Fat Boy; and he had set in motion, with this pretty lie, the countdown to End Times.

The Beast could fool the best of them, and he almost always got his way.

But maybe not this time.

Woof Say All!

Chapter Two

Mary Mbwembwe Says Good-Bye to a Very Old Friend

Mary Mbwembwe was in the kitchen when the old woman died. She was making the old woman a cup of chamomile tea. By the time she came back the old woman was entirely gone. Mary Mbwembwe put the teacup and saucer down on the nightstand. She leaned over and kissed the old woman on the forehead. Then she dressed the old woman in her favorite robe, the peacock-colored silk one with passionflowers painted on it. She fixed the old woman's hair. She arranged her arms into a tasteful impression of repose. She called the coroner, and after that she called the daughter. While she waited for the coroner and the daughter to arrive she cleaned the old woman's home until it was spic-and-span. By mid-afternoon her job was done. The coroner had come and gone. The hearse had driven up and two somberly dressed gentlemen had zippered the old woman's body into a bag and had taken it away reverently.

The daughter looked up from her texting as if surprised to see Mary Mbwembwe standing there. She wrote Mary Mbwembwe a check for two hundred dollars. She had never liked Mary Mbwembwe, and she was behaving rudely now, barely looking at her, and handing the check over at arms' length.

By this time Mary Mbwembwe had been caring for the old woman for seven years, in a town called Hemet, in the California desert, not far from the border. It was a town mostly populated with elderly John Wayne fans and their caregivers. Mary Mbwembwe forgave the daughter for her abrupt manner. The daughter had just lost a mother, after all. It was natural to resent the caregiver in such circumstances. Mary Mbwembwe did not mention that two hundred dollars was less than she was owed, or that she would be sleeping in her car that night. A friend had written to say that a brand new nursing home had opened in a town to the north, a place where they paid minimum wage plus benefits. So she had a backup plan. The daughter watched her gather her things together to be sure no silver or crystal made its way into her bag. Mary Mbwembwe did not resent her for it. She did not complain. Her belongings were not complicated. She did not take long to pack. Her car complained, though, wheezing and belching as she backed out and drove away.

Mary Mbwembwe would have gone to the old woman's funeral but she was not invited.

Just as she got on the highway and headed north Mary Mbwembwe checked her rear-view mirror, and in that very moment—in that casual, nostalgic look backward at her former life—she saw the beginning of all that was to come.

It came in the shape of a strange, sullen-yellow cloud, far to the south, still close to the horizon but billowing upwards, as if spores had just been released from the biggest puff-ball mushroom in the world.

The cloud didn't look to her like ordinary smog. It looked sinister and alive.

"Would you look at that," Mary Mbwembwe said.

Of course that old woman died a long time ago, so long ago that Mary Mbwembwe has since forgotten the old woman's name. It was a time when new wars were popping up on every continent, and vast sheets of ice were falling into the sea, and a third of the trees on the planet were burning. Korea still existed. Burkina Faso still existed. Countries with borders and names still existed. People still had hands with opposable thumbs, for the most part.

And on that day Mary Mbwembwe did not think of the world and its troubles. She was on a journey. The road was in front of her, not in her rear-view mirror. The sullen-yellow puff-ball mushroom cloud brooding on the horizon to the south would take care of itself, and if not, well then, there was no use worrying over what couldn't be helped, because everything that ever happened in this world was meant to be.

After reminding herself of all these things Mary Mbwembwe drove on with a hopeful heart.

Chapter Three

Josefina Guzman Meets
a Suspicious Fox

That same night, Josefina Guzman—who was, incidentally, a proud member of the Guzman branch of the Muwekma Ohlone Tribe—began to climb a ladder to the top of a shipping container, which was resting, slightly skewed, at the mucky end of the San Francisco Bay, far to the north of the spreading yellow haze along the border. The shipping container had come to rest at the end of a dirt path, on top of a defunded Superfund site, near a sewage treatment plant, in a township called Nethalem, formerly famous for its small craft harbor. Long ago the harbor had silted in, and now the only remnants of the harbor were the carcasses of abandoned boats, no longer seaworthy, lying at angles in the reeds and mud.

Josefina Guzman lived in the shipping container. She had set up a bed and a tiny table and chair for herself inside it. Also she had acquired some excellent Coleman-brand camping equipment, donated from the local parish. A stove. A torch. A catalytic space heater. Sometimes on clear nights Josefina Guzman would climb to the top of the shipping container to sleep, because the cool metal surface straightened out her back better than any chiropractor could. Also, she liked the view. Now that she had reached the top of the ladder she lay on her back and stared up at the sky. The moon was red and gibbous, and she cupped her hand under it, and imagined she was holding it.

Josefina Guzman's nearest neighbors lived in the village of Nethalem and their homes clustered around the little church, a dirt-path-mile away from her shipping container. Like her they were living in a flood plain, and barely scraping a living together, but they took care of her even so. Josefina Guzman was the parish's adoptive hard case. The parish priest's name was Father Juan del Rosario and he was from Argentina. Now and then Father Juan del Rosario would lead his congregants up the dirt path to Josefina Guzman's place and they would pray with her. She had a reputation for wisdom that came with her withered sun-dried features. To add to that reputation she wore seagull feathers in her hair.

It pleased her to live so close to the land. Of course the land probably belonged to someone, and the container too, and they would come one day and tell her to get lost. But maybe not. Maybe this was a completely abandoned container. And maybe the land was still classified as "water," here at the silted-in edge of things, so no one could really own it or take it away from her. It made her happy to think that a patch of new earth had risen up spontaneously from the mud and had escaped being surveyed and seized by the government and parceled off to the rich and powerful. This bit of land seemed protected by an unseen force for good. Sometimes she could see that unseen force, as a matter of fact, shimmering at the edges of her vision.

Or maybe it was her cataracts.

A sifting wind flowed through the reeds and it made the moon seem heavier in her hand than a moment ago, so she let the moon go.

Then it seemed as if she might have heard something in the reeds, something that whistled, or sang out.

Something caught in Josefina Guzman's heart.

But when she tried to listen more closely—when she tried to be sure she had heard anything at all—she only heard a pack of coyotes howling over by the freeway, where a new fire had apparently broken out, the way fires do, and it made the horizon in that direction glow a dull and brooding shade of orange.

Josefina Guzman decided she didn't want to sleep outside after all.

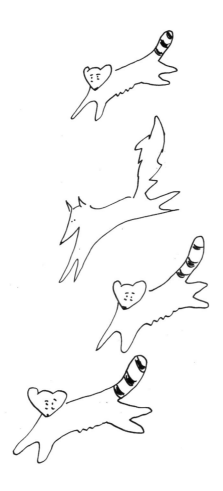

Just when both of Josefina Guzman's feet were safely back on the ground, some shapes made their way out of the muck and reeds. The shapes were trotting toward her. Her eyes were bad and she thought they were dogs until they stopped right in front of her: a fox and three raccoons, traveling together. Their eyes glowed. They nodded their small animal heads wisely. Josefina Guzman half-expected them to speak. Next she wondered if they were rabid. She wasn't sure whether to step toward them boldly to scare them off, or to run away. Before she could decide, the fox let out a cry that sounded like laughter and the four creatures ran away together into the dark.

"That's right, scat, get out of here," Josefina Guzman said.

But she felt disgruntled to be so easily dismissed by these creatures. Also it worried her to be talking out loud to animals. She was worried for her mind, because she was old. It took her a long time to fall asleep, because she was afraid her mind would be even less clear in the morning, and that she would be well on her way to becoming a ridiculous old woman. When she finally did fall asleep she had a dream about two bears, and a panther, and a pack of dogs, and a young girl with a baby in her arms; and the girl said to Josefina Guzman: "I'm looking for a boy named Lix Tetrax, do you know him?" and Josefina Guzman shook her head and said: "What nonsense, now leave me alone;" but the girl would not go away until Josefina Guzman woke up in the dark, and then—even though to be alone was what she had wanted all along—she somehow missed the girl, and was sorry that the girl had left so soon.

Chapter Four
Stella Steals Some Kitchen Shears

Stella's part in the story begins in the town of Barstow, on the night of the Yellow Puff-Ball Mushroom Cloud, which was, coincidentally for Stella, also the night when she finally decided to run away for good.

Stella was pregnant. Her mother was in jail. Her father was unknown. Her aunt would kick her out soon enough.

So as soon as everyone went to bed Stella stuffed all of her money into her underwear: the fifty-seven dollars that she had saved up honestly, plus the three twenties from the baby's father.

Into her L.L. Bean tote bag went some extra clothes.

Into her back pocket went the index card with the address of the baby's father written on it. The phone number had turned out to belong to somebody else, but the address was straight from his driver's license—she had copied it down herself after borrowing the three twenties from his wallet.

Just as she was going out the door, her baby's voice stopped her in her tracks.

TAKE THE KITCHEN SHEARS, her baby said.

"Why do I need to take the kitchen shears?" Stella said.

YOU'LL SEE, the baby said.

Stella was in a hurry so instead of arguing she went to the kitchen and grabbed her aunt's shears from the drawer and stuffed them into her bag.

TAKE THE GUN, TOO, the baby said.

"No gun," Stella said sternly.

She opened the front door and closed it softly behind her and took her first steps toward her fate, past her aunt's cactus garden, across the parking lot, and under the neon apartment sign, half-burned-out and sickly humming. She picked her way through a field full of broken bottles until she got to a barbed-wire fence. She pulled the wires apart and squeezed through. From there she followed the railroad tracks. Time sped up mysteriously. All of her sluggish regrets and random fears fell away. The tracks led her to another road and she took it. A blood-red moon was rising and it looked like a half-eaten, red Nilla Wafer.

At last she came to the part of town that was shaped like a grid, with sidewalks and streetlights. A block past the Rotten Robbie station she got to the Interstate, where she stood under the streetlight by the onramp with very good posture and waited for her ride to come along.

She could have made excuses about her behavior but she didn't. Ever since getting pregnant she had felt herself becoming ever more healthy and strong, day by day. She felt fecund. She felt blessèd. She felt feral. She felt like dropping to the ground and running on all fours and howling. The baby's father's name was Lix Tetrax and much of his body including his private parts had been sheathed in luxurious fur. To call Lix Tetrax hirsute did not do him justice. Making love with him had been like making love with a large plush toy. His teeth were small. His accent was foreign. His laugh was maniacal. He rode a Harley Soft Tail Fat Boy. He told her he worked for the Government, but which Government wasn't clear.

NETHALEM, YOU MUST GET TO NETHALEM, the baby chanted.

"All right, I'm going," she said, and wondered when her ride would come along.

Now you would think Stella would have asked herself now and then why her baby was so bossy, even in utero. You would think she would wonder about her baby's apparent command of more than one Indo-European language. You would think Stella might have wondered about the meanings of some of those comments her baby made, for instance: EGO SUM DOMINUS PESTIFER MUNDI, a favorite saying of her little babe, or: ETHDAY-ANDAY-AMNATION-DAY! which her baby would sing in a bell-like voice and in a playful little tune of the baby's own making.

But Stella took life as it came. Also she had fallen unconditionally in love with the little thing. She was going to love her baby no matter what its peculiarities. Sometimes when she was alone she would hold her baby and herself at the same time, wrapping her arms around their shared body, and she would sing pop songs from the radio to her baby, and the baby would sing back, using its own special words. How could it be otherwise? Did not every other mother feel the same way exactly?

THIS IS YOUR RIDE COMING UP NOW, the baby said. THE DRIVER'S NAME IS MARGIE PEACH. BE CAREFUL. SHE WILL WANT TO KNOW ALL YOUR BUSINESS

The car stopped.

"I'm Margie Peach and I breed whip-tail lizards," the woman behind the wheel said. "What are you doing? Why are you trying to catch a ride out here in the middle of the night? It seems unwise. Anybody could come along."

In spite of the woman's persnickety nosiness, Stella settled into her seat gratefully. She was tired of standing alone in the dark and making no progress toward her goal. She even made small talk, if a little spitefully, for as long as she could manage it, until she fell asleep.

Chapter Five
Margie Peach Follows a Giddy, Blood-Lust Scent

"Now, why is a young Black girl hitching a ride out of Barstow California, at this time of the night and in times like these?" was the first question in Margie Peach's head when she saw the girl standing by the side of the highway with one arm raised. Margie Peach wanted to know the answer badly enough that she pulled over. But she watched to make sure the girl didn't pick up a companion or two on her way to the car. She had heard stories about how young girls were used as bait, so when a kind and unsuspecting motorist stopped to help, here comes an ambush of men from the bushes, men with names like D-Money or Smoothie, to rape and to rob. Thankfully nobody jumped from the bushes this time. She unlocked the passenger-side door and the girl got in. Margie Peach locked the doors again. She flipped the dome light on to get a better look and thought: "Holy moly this girl is pregnant. Nine months at least. Maybe she's hitching a ride straight to the hospital. It wouldn't surprise me. This girl is bound to have a story. I, too, have a story."

"I wish you would turn that light off," the girl said. "Aren't we going to drive?"

"I'm Margie Peach and I breed whip-tail lizards," Margie Peach said. "What are you doing? Why are you trying to catch a ride out here in the middle of the night? It seems unwise. Anybody could come along."

"What's wrong with your eye?" the girl said.

"It's called strabismus," Margie said. "My type is called exotropia. It does not affect my driving in any way. I've adapted."

"What about your hands?"

"I think you are a very impertinent girl."

"I'm just asking," the girl said. "I guess most people don't ask. I guess most people just stare."

"It's called arthrogryposis," Margie said. "Maybe you should get another ride."

"My baby thinks you're all right," the girl said.

"That so," Margie said.

"Yes it is," the girl said. "Do you want to give me a ride, or not?"

"I don't know why I'd stop if I didn't intend to give you a ride," Margie said.

Margie turned the dome light off. She put the car in gear and pulled back on the highway.

"I'm going to Nethalem," the girl said. "It's on the bay. My boyfriend went on ahead. His name is Lix Tetrax and he's expecting me. He'll be happy to see me, that's for sure."

"Mm, hmm," Margie said. "I guess he misses you."

"Yes, he does."

The girl said these last words as if daring Margie Peach to challenge her. Margie let it go.

"I'm going to San Francisco, myself," she said. "When I get there I'm going to stay at the famous Intercontinental Hotel. I'm going to drink a Cherry Coke at the Top of the Mark. It's been my dream in life ever since I saw it in a movie and now that I've lost my job I'm going to do it before I run out of money and never have the chance. I can get you pretty close to where you're going, I guess."

"Whatever," the girl said, and yawned.

Margie Peach did not feel rebuffed. She was used to people being rude to her. She forgave the girl right away. Because, after all, wouldn't anyone be a little short-tempered if they happened to find themselves enormously pregnant, alone in the dark, and hundreds of miles away from where they wanted to be? Margie wanted to help. She resolved to keep asking the girl questions. She wanted to know the girl's story. Maybe there would be time to tell the girl her own story, too. But before Margie could think of how to begin the conversation, the girl had fallen asleep.

Margie didn't even know her name.

She slapped on the radio. The voice of the President came on. He was giving a speech. Margie turned it up loud enough for the President's stuffy-summer-cold voice to wake the Dead.

The girl slept on.

Margie turned the radio off.

With nothing left to do, Margie began to tell herself her own story, in her head. She never seemed to get it exactly right. She was always making herself out to be the hero or the villain.

They were coming up on the infamous town of San Bernardino.

Margie Peach woke the girl with a shake to the shoulder. She felt taken advantage of by this pregnant, sullen girl. She felt like an unpaid chauffeur.

"Welcome to San Bernardino," she said. "I need a break."

"Just let me out when you get off the highway," the girl said.

"No," Margie said. "You could use a break too. No one is going to come along at this time of night. Look, there's no other traffic except for truckers and believe me you want to avoid that sort. I'll buy you a meal. I can do that. It's the least I can do. It's no trouble at all. We're going the same way. You shouldn't be out in the dark, a young girl in your condition. You shouldn't be wandering around in the middle of the night. The world isn't safe."

"It'll be light soon. Just let me out at the exit."

"It's no trouble," Margie said, and patted the girl's knee in a way she meant to be reassuring.

"Let me out this second," the girl said, and she opened the door, just a little but as they were speeding along at seventy the wind howled through the crack and the car veered left.

"Stop that, shut the door!" Margie said.

The girl pulled the door shut but she kept hold of the handle.

"Here's the exit," the girl said. "Slow down, slow down."

Margie slowed down. She used her turn signal. She exited the highway smoothly.

"Look, there's a sign for a Denny's," Margie said. "They're always open. Come on. I'll buy you a blueberry waffle and a Dr. Pepper and then we can go on. I should have a coffee myself. I want to help you. It's stupid to be standing in the dark when God knows what is out there."

Margie Peach drove as gently as she could so she wouldn't alarm the girl again. She drove right up to the front entrance of the Denny's. She could see the waitress, a kindly-looking woman with an enormous bustline, and she was topping off the coffee for a customer sitting by the window.

The girl got out.

"Just tell me your name at least!" Margie Peach said.

"Stella," the girl said, and then she slammed the door and went inside without looking back. Her lack of gratitude made Margie feel cynical.

"I sure could use a pit stop after all this driving," Margie thought. "I should go right in there and buy myself a coffee. It's still a couple of hours until dawn. A coffee would do me good. I deserve a rest. I don't need to sit with Stella."

But Margie felt hurt and unappreciated, so instead of going inside she backed out and kept going.

Soon she began to regret it. She had been driving too long and she was tired and her strabismus was acting up. She had begun to see double again.

Oddly enough as her vision grew more impaired, her sense of smell improved. She could smell very well indeed. She could smell the exhaust fumes coming in through her closed window. She could smell the remains of a strawberry milkshake she had spilled in the front seat of her car three years ago. She could smell her own body. Her hands lost their grip on the steering wheel—no longer could she grasp the wheel with any strength at all—and the car began to swerve. Pull over, pull over, she told herself. The shoulder was wide. She pulled over and cut the engine. She opened her door and flopped out, barely able to stand. As a matter of fact she could not stand any longer. She dropped to her knees, or to her paws, rather, and she ran from the car without a second thought and into the grassy field next to the highway, and she was happy, and she kept running, running, her throat and mouth and body filled with the giddy blood-lust scent of the sixteen cows asleep in the high grass a mile away.

The rest of the night was a blur.

Chapter Six
Major Eureka Yamanaka Does Her Duty

That same night, a woman by the name of Major Eureka Yamanaka—a fourth-generation Californian and a third-generation Air Force officer—found herself hefting the nuclear football up into Marine Helicopter Squadron One, in Las Vegas, right after the President had climbed in.

The nuclear football was a briefcase. The briefcase weighed forty-five pounds and it looked like a prop from a movie made a long time ago. Inside it was the portable means for the President to launch a nuclear-style Armageddon.

Major Eureka Yamanaka climbed in and buckled up.

The helicopter lifted off.

The lights of the city fell away and they flew toward the desert dark.

"Thank you again, Generals, for your quick work," the President said. "So who was it this time?"

The President's voice sounded hollow because he was wearing a gas mask. They were all wearing gas masks. The President's flowing-red, lustrous, virile, and Samson-like hair—the envy of all other men (especially men who were forced to wear comb-overs, or to endure painful surgeries implanting unconvincing hair plugs into their scalps, or who pretended to love their bald pates while secretly feeling impotent and powerless)—was matted with worry, and it stuck out at the sides of his gas mask like a scrubby ruff.

"After we received this latest intel, sir, we thought it best to remove your person from the vicinity," one of the men said, and then he flipped open his secure and ruggedized secret computer with a flourish. Major Eureka Yamanaka watched the screen, too, over the President's shoulder. She saw a grainy, black-and-white drone feed of two border patrol officers in uniform. They were standing next to their patrol car. They appeared to be on a cigarette break. The two of them were looking off in the distance while taking long drags on their unfiltered fags. Then one of them stubbed out his butt with vigor and began to look through a pair of binoculars instead. A few seconds later he dropped his binoculars and clutched at his throat. His jaw appeared to lengthen. He appeared to choke and gag. He looked like a poorly executed horror-movie effect and his acting was overdone. The other man tried to help but seconds later he convulsed in exactly the same way as his partner. Major Eureka Yamanaka watched the men's incisors sharpen. She saw their skin over-fur itself. Within seconds, in the place of two young border patrol officers, there stood two young coyotes.

The coyotes sniffed the ground and ran off-camera.

"What the Hell?" the President said.

"Exactly the word for it, sir. We have unconfirmed reports of an unidentified toxic event, seventy-one miles from where these men were standing. We think the two events are related. We can't rule out the possibility that the country is under chemical attack."

Somebody's phone rang.

"The Governor of California is asking whether to evacuate the state," somebody said.

"Too late for that," the President said. "Those people are doomed."

No one said anything. They were thinking about the doomed people. Their gas masks made them look like a cluster of praying mantises.

"They must have hacked our feeds," said one of the Generals. "Because what we saw there, well, those things can't happen in reality."

"You people give me a headache," the President said. "They hacked our feeds? Why am I in this helicopter? Why do I have this gas mask on? Why are you evacuating me to a secure facility? I need a drink. Get me some gin, straight up from the bottle. How do you drink through a gas mask?"

"Your mask has a built-in hydration tube, sir," one of the men said helpfully. The President was a famous drinker and so they were prepared. One of them brought out a bottle of Beefeater from his briefcase. After a while they all decided to test their hydration tubes. They passed around the bottle. They all agreed the Beefeater tasted flat, which was natural, because they couldn't smell anything through their gas masks. When the bottle came her way Major Eureka Yamanaka took a swig through her tube. "Allll...right...Major!" they drawled. They were oafish clods. She confused them, not just because she was female, but also because she was Japanese-American, and lastly because she was Californian. An hour later they touched down at the Mountain and they climbed into armored Humvees and sprawled out, squeezing her and the football into a tiny corner. They rode a mile straight into the Mountain. The blast doors opened and they drove in and the doors closed behind. They made their way down a concrete tunnel to the Command Center, where two hundred soldiers were busy at their workstations, each piloting a drone that hovered thousands of feet above a target of interest. On the big screen in front, the World Map kept blinking as new parts lit up. The place felt completely familiar to Major Eureka Yamanaka, from the movies.

A general in fatigues strode up and saluted the President.

"We are protected by state-of-the-art air filters here in this facility, sir," the general said. "One hundred percent. State of the art. Installed last month. Lucky thing. You can take your gas masks off now, men."

Chapter Seven
Wanda Lubiejewski Learns the True Meaning of the Word "Homewrecker"

The door at the Denny's banged open and Wanda Lubiejewski—a woman whose only crazy dream in life was to get breast reduction surgery one day—looked up from the cash register and thought: "That girl looks like she is going to have a baby right this minute, on my shift."

The girl made her way past Wanda Lubiejewski with ballsy nonchalance and disappeared into the ladies room. No worries, Wanda decided. The girl wasn't barefoot. She wasn't breaking any health codes. She wasn't visibly in labor. Wanda Lubiejewski looked at her watch. She decided to give the girl five minutes' privacy before she'd go check on her.

The girl came out in three minutes with her L.L. Bean tote bag slung over her shoulder like she was on her way to a slumber party.

"One? Sit anywhere you want."

The girl found a booth and sat in it. Wanda Lubiejewski followed her with a menu.

"I want a beer. I want a bowl of chili too."

"We have beer, but no chili tonight," Wanda Lubiejewski said. "We're out. Do you really think you should be drinking beer in your condition? How old are you anyway?"

"Don't treat me like a kid," the girl said. "My boyfriend rides a Harley Soft Tail Fat Boy."

"You sound ridiculous," Wanda Lubiejewski said.

"I'll have a hot chocolate with whipped cream," the girl said.

29

Someone was waiting at the register to pay his check and Wanda Lubiejewski went back and rang him up and paid the man his change. She dispensed hot chocolate from the dispenser. At the last minute she embellished the top with a mound of extra whipped cream. But the girl didn't notice. Her head was down on the table and her eyes were closed. She looked asleep, or maybe done in by events. Wanda Lubiejewski put the hot chocolate down gently in front of her and walked back over by the cash register and bought herself a pack of LifeSavers from under the counter and ate one.

Elsie, the other waitress on shift, came over and stood next to her.

They both watched the girl for a while.

"It's weird, the way she's coming in here alone this time of night," Elsie said.

"It's not so weird," Wanda Lubiejewski said.

Elsie went to clear some tables. Wanda Lubiejewski filled the saltshakers and the ketchup bottles and the syrups. She did the work slowly because she knew there would soon be nothing to do except wait for her shift to be over. The USA Todays arrived. Wanda took a paper to the break room and poured herself a coffee. She could hear Marvin in the kitchen slowly scraping the grill to get it ready for the breakfast shift: scrape, scrape.

Elsie came in the break room and lit a cigarette, even though it was against the rules.

"No ring on her finger," Elsie said.

"That doesn't mean anything," Wanda Lubiejewski said.

Elsie turned on the television. The President was on. He was giving a speech.

OUR ENEMY CARRIES OUT ONE UNTHINKABLE ATROCITY AFTER ANOTHER. TONIGHT THEY ATTACKED OUR COUNTRY WITH A CHEMICAL WEAPON. WE CANNOT LET THIS EVIL CONTINUE. WE WILL NOT DEFEAT IT WITH CLOSED EYES, OR SILENCED VOICES. I ALONE CAN SAVE YOU

"Blah, blah blah, every time I see that man on the TV he makes it sound like the end of the world," Elsie said, and shook her head. "My husband loves him. He says the election was Divine Will. I say to him, 'Honey, it's only Divine Will if God thinks it's Apocalypse Time.'"

"Apocalypse Time," Wanda Lubiejewski said. "That sounds like a beer commercial. I'm going to check the restrooms. You better get out front again, I guess."

Someone in the men's room had missed the urinal by a mile, as usual, and there were random lengths of TP scattered all over the wet floor. One of the toilets was stopped up. She plunged the toilet and she mopped the floor and after that she bleached all of the toilets and wiped the mirror down with a rag. The woman's room wasn't too bad but she brought it into perfect order, and then she took the trash out back to the dumpster. The air outside was warmer than it was inside. Being outside reminded Wanda Lubiejewski that she was always breathing indoor air full of grease while on the job, and the grease would settle into her clothes and onto her skin, so that when her shift was done she'd smell like fried things, and need to go home and shower and wash her clothes twice.

Her husband worked the day shift at Home Depot and they only had an hour together every morning, before he left for work. They usually passed the time in different rooms, unless he had something urgent to complain about. While waiting for his wife to improve herself, her husband had found a new, more pliant help-meet, and Wanda Lubiejewski knew it, but whenever she presented him with an unfamiliar charge on the credit card, from a restaurant he had never taken her to, or a hotel she had never heard of, he would raise his voice and call her a "homewrecker," which confused her—wasn't he the homewrecker?—and she would drop it.

Thinking of her domestic troubles made her feel pressure in her chest, though, so she stopped thinking and went back inside and washed her hands and then she made her way out front.

Just before dawn the pregnant girl ordered an All American Slam. Wanda Lubiejewski took the order. Marvin, the cook, nearly sleeping in front of the grill, made the eggs and bacon and pancakes. Elsie served them.

The sun rose through a yellow haze and Wanda knew the day was going to be a scorcher.

"You won't get a cent out of that girl," Elsie said, before she left for the night, and Wanda said: "I'll cover it, then, and your tip too, if you want."

She decided to check the restrooms again. When she got back a California Highway Patrol car was pulling up in the parking lot. She looked over at the pregnant girl's booth and it was empty. The girl had left a twenty on the table, though. Wanda rang her up and put the change in her pocket to give to Elsie later, for a tip. The officers sat at the counter and ordered regular coffee and apple pie, same as always. In spite of the blast of Old Spice they had brought in with them, the two officers looked like they hadn't shaved in days, and a ragged smell came from their clothes, as if they'd been sleeping in the woods.

The day manager showed up twenty minutes late. Wanda Lubiejewski was glad to see him because she wasn't feeling well at all. By the time she drove up to her two-bedroom, one-bath house (double-mortgaged, underwater) she just managed to kill the engine and open the car door and climb out before a dizzy spell overtook her. She lumbered toward her front door. Her next-door neighbor came out of his house for the newspaper and, seeing Wanda, ran back inside without it. Wanda tripped on her daughter's tricycle and picked herself up again. Her bones ached and her broad black snout was running. She felt terrible. Once she got inside she would call the doctor first thing. But the thought of calling a doctor sent her into a panic about her annual insurance deductible. Maybe after she took a nap she wouldn't need a doctor after all.

But she could not open the door.

The round knob kept slipping, too small for her mitts to grab.

She yelled for her husband to come help her: "Howie, Howie, let me come in!"

She finally managed to ring the doorbell with her snout.

Her daughter opened the door and ran away.

At least her girl had left the heavy wooden front door ajar. Wanda pushed on the screen door, gently. She was relieved to see that the screen door crumpled easily, with one swipe of the paw, and she was inside. She saw her husband coming toward her. He was angry with her again, and she deserved it. Her husband looked mysteriously beautiful to her, while she, Wanda Lubiejewski, was a fat ugly beast. She saw the truth of it. No wonder he had found himself a girlfriend. Who could blame him? Her husband's gun was in his hand and he was pointing it. "I'm sorry, I'm sorry, I'm sorry," she tried to say. She was taken aback by the violent powerful sounds coming out of her. She didn't sound apologetic at all. All at once she felt strong, in new and surprising ways. She began to understand that she was important in her own right, and that she had nothing to apologize for, and indeed that she was destined to become one of the heroes of this story. She discovered that she was charging toward the man with the gun. With a gathering explosive muscular force she bounded straight into him—the bullets barely grazing her fur—and ran on through the house and out the back door—smashing the walls to each side as she ran, on account of her powerful girth—and she was free.

Wanda Lubiejewski stopped.

She swiveled her great head toward the splintered back wall of her home and thought: "I need to save my little girl."

She ran back through the broken wall and over the little man lying in the hallway with his gun. She crashed through more walls. The ceilings sagged inward like big hammocks, and there was rubble and dust in the air—she had wrecked this home entirely—and it didn't matter because she found her daughter safe in her little bedroom, sitting on her own little bed and reading her favorite book, as if she had been waiting all along for her mother to come rescue her. Wanda Lubiejewsi cradled the girl gently in her jaws and then she busted out the back wall of her daughter's bedroom, and ran on, thinking: "Will you look at that," and: "I wish my mother could see me now," and most of all: "I have always known I was a bear," a feeling so self-affirming that she snorted with pleasure, loud enough to set the car alarms off, all up and down the street.

Book Two

Therianthropy

Chapter Eight
Margie Peach Learns All About "Agent-T"

At dawn Margie Peach happened upon a puddle and, after lapping from it, looked down at the reflection in the calming water, and thought: "I'm a dog."

She knew this particular thought was impossible, though, both because dogs were not self-aware, and because dogs could not recognize their own reflection.

From one moment to the next she forgot a thought, and thought another.

This next thought was: "I'm hungry."

And then she thought: "Wait a minute. I'm a common, ordinary dog. What I really should be thinking about is, why am I a dog?"

She thought about it three or four or five seconds and then a sharp sweet scent caught her attention and with a violent compulsive swerve of her head to bring her nose closer to the source of that pungent arresting smell she saw the flicker of a face, a vole, or a rat, and the smell and face compelled her to bray and run after it.

She didn't catch it though.

Winded, panting, she flopped down in the shade of an old eucalyptus tree and fell asleep.

"I'm hungry," Margie Peach thought, and was awake.

"Wait a minute, I'm a dog," she thought.

She tried and failed to feel alarm.

"I don't feel alarm," she finally admitted to herself, "because in my heart of hearts and soul of souls I know it has always been the right thing for me, Margie Peach, to be a dog, and how good it is to finally be exactly what I am meant to be!"

But she was a rational dog, and she knew for a fact she couldn't actually, literally be a dog, and so, just to be sure she was still herself, and not a dog at all, she recited a passage of a beloved poem, a habit of hers.

And on the pedestal, these words appear:
My name is Ozymandias, King of Kings;
Look on my Works, ye Mighty, and despair!
Nothing beside remains. Round the decay
Of that colossal Wreck, boundless and bare
The lone and level sands stretch far away."

Margie Peach took stock of her situation. She was herself. She was a dog. And all around her the smell of the wild bright world kept changing: from the slow, cold, solid scents of hay and citrus blossom in the morning, to the ragged heated bursts of loam and manure and carrion and diesel fuel in the afternoon, and on into the night, with its smell of garbage in the cans, and gunpowder, and blood.

The dog sprang up and began to trot along joyfully, in search of food and companionship.

She set off instinctively back toward the smell of cars and humans. As she traveled she thought: "How interesting that my dog self naturally wants to find the company and protection of humans, who will shelter me and feed me."

She avoided crossing roads and highways but she risked crossing a parking lot behind a Cattlemen's Steakhouse, where her nose led her to a dumpster filled and overflowing. A Great Dane was at the dumpster, tearing through plastic garbage bags that had spilled onto the ground, to find the bones, the meat. The larger dog allowed Margie to share in the feast. The other dog even said—or did Margie imagine it?—"Hell, yes, why the Hell not, there's plenty here for both of us."

"Excuse me," Margie Peach said. "But did you speak?"

"Good Lord, can this dumb beast understand me?" the Great Dane said, and began to whimper, and then to growl and bare its teeth.

"I'm not a dumb beast," Margie Peach said. "I'm Margie Peach."

"You're a goddamn dog," the other dog said. "And I am not a goddamn dog. This is my dream. This is my nightmare."

"I can see your point," Margie Peach said. "I was on my way to San Francisco. I was planning to stay at the Intercontinental Hotel and to drink a Cherry Coke at the Top of the Mark. No doubt my credit card has been charged for the day while I find myself eating meaty garbage with you as company."

She was unable to read the Great Dane's expression.

The Great Dane began to bite its hindquarters, worrying at a place that was already hairless and bleeding.

"Look, that's not so good for you," Margie Peach said. "You've opened the skin. You could get an infection."

The other dog sat down abruptly.

"I want to wake up now," the dog said pleadingly.

Margie Peach wanted to help.

"All right," Margie Peach said. "But let's begin by making this a better dream."

She sniffed through the garbage until she found what she was looking for: a T-bone with most of the meat still clinging to it. She dropped it in front of the other dog, and watched the dog eat.

"There you go," Margie Peach said. "Nothing is so bad on a full stomach."

When the other dog was done, Margie Peach said: "Come on, let's go now. I'll take you somewhere safe, away from cars and lights."

She no longer thought that seeking human company would be the right thing to do, given the Great Dane's fragility. No doubt humans would treat the Great Dane as if she were a dog, and would upset the Great Dane because of it. So Margie Peach began to trot softly back the way she had come, toward the comfort of the eucalyptus tree under which she had slept that morning. The larger dog followed. "Could it be that I am an alpha dog?" Margie thought. "Could it be that I am a leader of dogs?" And the thought pleased her, and made her feel conversational.

"How did your dream begin?" she asked the Great Dane, as they loped.

"In my waking life I'm not a dog," the Great Dane said. "In my waking life I'm Dr. Alberta Chen and I work at the Center for Disease Control. My dream began when I was assigned to collect and test a sample of a therianthropic chemical agent released last night at the border."

"Therianthropic chemical agent?" Margie said. "Last night?"

"That's right. We named it Agent-T. We think it was meant for Las Vegas. The President gave a speech there last night. He was the likely target. Or it could be a toxic chemical spill of our own making, just an accident. It doesn't matter where it came from. We're doomed. The wind has done the job. We had reports of infection coming in from as far north as Portland and as far east as St. Louis. Skepticism has bought us time before the inevitable chaos and terror to come. No one can believe it's really happening."

"What is really happening?" Margie Peach said.

"A therianthropic chemical agent," the doctor said tiredly. "It turns people into mindless beasts. Women are especially susceptible. The Y chromosome gives men some resistance to the agent's brutish effects. Some people seem to resist for hours or days while others succumb to their beastly natures on contact with the gas. If we had more time we could have identified the resistance factors. We could have developed a vaccine. I became infected myself while trying to isolate Agent-T in the lab. A colleague tried to shoot me but he turned into a macaw before he could manage it, and I made my escape."

"Your dream sounds very far-fetched," Margie said, and rejected it.

"You are an ignorant brute animal without the capacity to speculate on what is to come. The Generals will want to retaliate even if we don't find an enemy to blame. Even if it's one of our own DARPA projects, run amok. The Generals will convince the President to bomb Mexico. Maybe even California itself."

"Don't get carried away. That would never happen," Margie said. "It's not going to happen. Everything is going to be all right. You should stop worrying about things you can't control. We're helpless dogs in this world and nothing more, after all."

For a moment the Great Dane seemed to accept it. She lolled her tongue and they began to lope along peacefully together, and the odors on the breeze drew them both forward, until the Great Dane stopped abruptly.

"Oh God, oh God, oh God," she said. "Don't you see, the Enemy has already won. Look at you. Look at me. It's the perfect weapon. We won't be able to strike back with paws for hands. We can't use a gun or a phone. We won't be able to defend ourselves, or to warn the American People."

"Don't worry, Dr. Chen. Please. I'm sure it will work out in the end."

"We're helpless," the Great Dane insisted. "Imagine trying to launch missiles or fire weapons with claws and paws and snouts. They will mow us down like dumb dogs."

"We aren't dumb, in either sense of the word," Margie Peach observed.

Dr. Alberta Chen had begun to bite her hindquarters again. Margie waited patiently. She spoke soothingly. "There, there, Doctor," she said, and: "It can't be all bad, can it?" She tried comforting the other dog with a friendly snuffle, and then a tender nip, but the Great Dane turned on her, lashing out, biting into Margie Peach's shoulder and barking: "Go away! Leave me alone!"

"Now just hold on a minute," Margie Peach said. Her fur was thick and the bite hadn't reached through to her skin but the gesture had stung her.

"No, I mean it, go away, you don't belong at all," the Great Dane insisted. "You're the problem. You keep confusing me so I can't wake up. Go! Get out of here!"

"Please, Doctor," Margie Peach said. "You are a scientist. Let's be rational."

But the other woman kept trying to sink her teeth into Margie Peach, and eventually Margie Peach gave up. She loped back toward light and civilization, alone again. Once in a while she looked around, hopeful that the Great Dane might have changed her mind and would be following, but the other dog was far behind her now, still busy worrying her hindquarters in a frenzied attempt to force herself to wake up by inflicting pain and self-injury, until Margie could no longer see her.

Margie Peach went on.

After a while she thought no more of the Great Dane, except to say to herself: "So then, my strange transformation has an explanation, and the explanation is scientific, and it has to do with verifiable causes, while all this time I had been thinking that it was my special fate to be a dog, and that my transformation was pre-ordained. Indeed I should be happy to learn that my condition is medical and reversible, one assumes, when one is given the proper antidote, but all I feel is sadness, to know that I am not so special after all."

And next she thought: "Funny, it seems to be the case that, now that I am a dog, I can only live in the moment, without worrying too long about my future or my immediate past, and what's more, without worrying what any man might think of me, or how I might be judged and found flawed and unattractive. In much the same way that our great Religions teach us, I have become mindful of the present. As a dog such a practice seems to come easily. Look at me, I have stopped worrying about that Great Dane altogether."

Then she felt bad about herself, though, to have stopped worrying about the Great Dane so easily, and for a while as she loped she gave into her long habit of thinking obsessively about her many flaws, which now included a lack of sufficient empathy for Dr. Alberta Chen.

Then this latest train of thought also faded, and the only thing she thought about was the new smell she was traveling toward. Smell was granular in a way she had not understood before. It came to her in bursts of physical awareness, as if some physical thing had been breathed in through her nostrils, and now circulated itself within her body, making her ears perk up and filling her mind with pictures. She smelled gasoline and wood smoke, and a tinge of sulfur dioxide, and jet fuel, and methane from cows, and also, swirling about and between these solid familiar smells, she smelled an indefinable, mysterious, dervish-like smell, one that Margie Peach could only suppose was Agent-T.

" 'I have never slept with a man before,' Margie Peach thought. "

At dawn she came upon a man lying under a piece of cardboard next to a road. She smelled his loneliness. Even though his whistle did not attract her, she approached the lonely man, and, seeing welcome in his eyes, stretched her length along his side, and licked his tears, and whined with him when he cried.

"I have never slept with a man before," Margie Peach thought. "And I never thought that I would have the chance, after living so long without any man wanting me. But look how our hearts are beating together. I have offered him love and companionship, along with the warmth of my body, and he gives me the same in return. I believe this is the way it must feel to be married, day upon day, and year upon year, living and sleeping together through every trial imaginable, and then one day you discover that the decades of your life have all been lived, and you are old, and you are still together, even after disappointing one another time and time again, and even after having lived a mediocre life full of sorrow, rather than the perfect, meaningful life you had imagined for yourself; and you have stayed together through it all, still keeping faith in what it means to love, and be loved, forever and ever."

But she couldn't get comfortable, and the man kept complaining about her odor and about his troubles, and so, after trying her best, she began to feel that she had not missed out on anything grand in life after all, to have never been close to a man, and she left him and went searching for the place where she could feel content, and where she could know that she was loved.

44

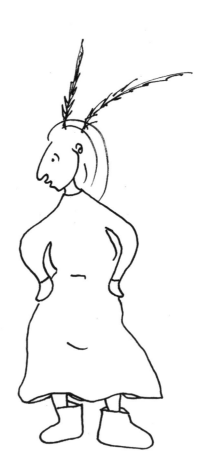

Chapter Nine

Josefina Guzman Disturbs
a Perfectly Round White Stone

At dawn Josefina Guzman woke up in her shipping container to the sound of trumpets booming out from the heavens.

Or maybe it was thunder.

Or maybe—she reconsidered as she woke more fully—it was the screeching of seabirds, combined with the barreled yelps of sea lions, along with the many other sounds of crying animals, mixing together in the air all around, a noise that reminded her that, even here at the edge of things, she was not alone.

Josefina Guzman crawled out of bed and grabbed her fishing pole in one hand and her bucket and net in the other. The sun was already bright and it pulled the day sharply into focus, and the air seemed to jangle and shiver from the noise of all the crying, screeching animals. Something happened now and then to make the animals come—a quirk of tide, a storm to the north—who knows?—and the fishing that morning was bound to be good. When she got closer to the edge of the bay, her boots began to make a splatting, sticky sound as she lifted each foot. She curled her toes inside her boots and held on, so a boot wouldn't get left behind in a suck of mud. When she got to the water's edge she could see why the birds were excited. Thousands of fish—anchovies, sardines, mackerel—swarmed in the shallows. The surface of the water was a glittering silver wonder. Seagulls and pelicans and loons were dipping and diving into that mass of fish, while sea lions had hauled themselves up on the weathered dock and were basking there, too gluttoned to care about the fish flapping on the surface of the water, just inches from their jaws.

Josefina Guzman's first thought was to scoop up some fish in her net. But then she saw scores of crabs, each the size of a basketball, crawling up out of the water, lively and huge and rushing toward her as if begging to be eaten. She grabbed the two closest crabs by their back legs and carried them back to her camp and built a fire and boiled them right up for breakfast, cracking them on the rocks and taking the best, meaty parts in her fingers to eat.

When she was done she licked her fingers and picked up her bucket and net. No need for her fishing pole on a day like this, when she could almost grab a catch with her bare hands. She made her way back through the reeds to the shore. Once there, she looked out across the bay, to the north, where she often saw sailboats and fishing boats out on the water. That morning she didn't see any. There weren't any trains or cars making their way along the edges of the bay, either. There was no human movement anywhere. It was as if the cacophonous throng of non-human life surrounding her—the gasping, dying fish in the shallows, the shrieking exultation of birds, the languid barking of sea lions—had taken up all of the space meant for living things.

The wind changed.

Josefina Guzman felt unsettled, and she didn't know why.

She decided that she didn't want to catch fish after all. The crabs were enough.

Back home she shut the sounds of the birds and sea creatures out of her mind. She cleaned up from her morning meal. She put the crab shells in a paper bag and walked into the reeds and tossed the shells there. She stripped down to her underwear and washed her clothes in the bucket and hung them on a line. The sun was strong, and it didn't take long for her clothes to dry.

That afternoon she swept the dirt around her shipping container with her straw broom. As she did so, she found a small and perfectly round white stone that intrigued her. She put it in her pocket for safekeeping.

Later, though, the stone began to bother her, there in her pocket. It weighed her down on one side, and it slapped against her thigh when she walked. So she took the stone out and tossed it on the ground, where it rolled in circles for a long time, much longer than it was reasonable for any stone to roll, until it found a spot that pleased it, where it rested.

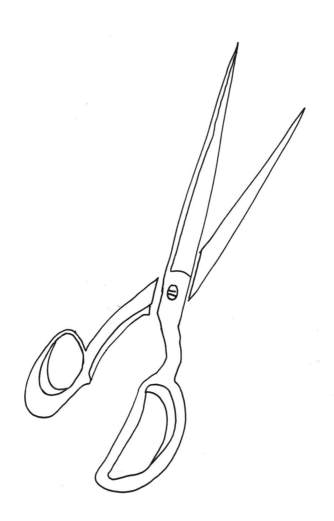

Chapter Ten
Stella Buys a Pack of Hostess Donettes

At dawn Stella strode with pretend confidence along a highway and waited for her next ride to come along. She was angry at herself because instead of waiting for a ride by the side of the road she had stuffed herself all night at the San Bernardino Denny's with eggs and pancakes and hot chocolate, and bacon, and now she felt discouraged by life, and tired of being pregnant. She tried some positive thinking. She told herself that she was beautiful in just the right ways and that she was going to be one helluva mother. She still had over a hundred dollars in her underwear. Dawn was raw at the edges and the air smelled fresh and washed clean. Small birds were frolicking and flocking in the air. Life at the moment was rich and full of promise. So of course the very first vehicle she saw coming down the road was a Dodge Ram pickup with a driver slowing down for her.

DON'T GET IN THE TRUCK. THE DRIVER IS A SOLDIER FOR THE OTHER SIDE, her baby said.

"You don't know anything," Stella said. "This is America. There is no other side." She was tired of being bossed around, most of all by her kid.

She walked up to the truck and looked in.

An old man, older than old, with pale blue veins beneath his pale white cheeks, and his shirt was clean and tucked in.

NO, said the baby.

"Why, hullo there, Missy," the man said through his open window. "Looks like you are going my way today. Hop in."

Stella did. She kept her bag on her lap just in case, her right hand inside it, gripping the kitchen shears.

They started off.

"Watcha got there in the bag?" the man said.

"Nothing."

"Okay, I don't care," the man said. "Just being friendly. Just making conversation."

"Okay."

The man slowed down a little, then looked at her, and then sped up again.

"I didn't see you was pregnant to begin with," he said.

Stella laughed.

"No, really," the man said. "Me, I'm a face man. I always look at the face first. Not the bodies. Not anything like that. Women love me for that. I never judge their shape."

I WARNED YOU, the baby said.

"Like, say, some other man might say to you, wow, girl, wow, do you have nice jugs," said the man. "I mean because your jugs are so nice and full and your skin so brown and warm. Your jugs are bigger than usual for a girl your frame. May I just touch one?"

"I have a pair of kitchen shears in my hand, pointing at you," Stella said.

"Oh, ha-ha," the old man said. "You do, do you. No harm, no harm. I'm just admiring."

Stella kept a grip on the shears and faced the window, looking out. She ignored her baby when it began to crow and shriek and mock and whistle. It was a beautiful day, and nothing too bad had happened yet, and the old man seemed to be respectful of her kitchen shears. There were streaks of sky peeking out between bright yellow clouds and there were Joshua trees as far as the eye could see. Looking at the Joshua trees flash by her window kaleidoscopically made her feel dizzy, and so she began to follow the telephone wires strung from

pole to pole as they dipped and swayed while they drove along, and—
that was funny—now she noticed there were birds flocking in the sky,
masses of them, flying in the same direction that they were driving,
almost as if leading her somewhere, and their wings beat in time with
the car wheels clacking along on the road beneath.

"This here is where you get out, Missy," the old man said. "You are
not the woman I thought you was. I've been looking for a new woman.
My old lady is a dog. She run off with my best friend. You looked
to me like you were looking for a friend yourself. You're welcome to
come along if I have misjudged you. I know some people."

"No thank you," Stella said.

"Well all right then. Hold onto your knickers. I meant no harm."

"Yeah. Okay. Thanks for explaining."

The old man seemed not so bad now. He was old and fragile, and
deserving of her pity. He was just a sad old man. She wondered if she
had misjudged him, and if he had just been trying to be friendly all
along, and if she had somehow signaled by her own behavior, or by
the clothes she was wearing, that his comments would be welcome.
She thought about apologizing. It wouldn't do any harm to thank him
for the ride. He had stopped for her, after all. He hadn't touched her
one bit.

"You are nothing more than a disgusting, nasty girl, of very low
intelligence, and you will not prevail," the old man said as he slowed
down. "After all it was not Adam, but the Woman who was in league
with Satan. Sin and damnation was the result and now your kind
squirts out murderers and rapists. But your time will soon be over,
Missy. America is Great and God is with us."

He was pulling over now and she hopped out and slammed the
door behind her just before his truck stopped all the way.

"Whore of Babylon, we will defeat you and your devil spawn," the
old man said, out his window, euphorically, and he drove away in a
spin of gravel.

IT COULD HAVE BEEN WORSE, the baby said. GOOD THING YOU LISTENED TO ME ABOUT THE KITCHEN SHEARS AT LEAST

And that is how Stella found herself in a place called Kramer's Korner, which was not much more than a crossroads in the high California desert. There was a Texaco station. There was a very tall sign that said "Kramer's Korner" on it. There was an endless sea of stubby underbrush stretching out in every direction and as far as the eye could see. That was about it. Stella second-guessed the wisdom of accepting a ride that had taken her far away from any major highway but she brightened when the very first vehicle she saw coming down the road was an eighteen-wheeler that she knew somehow was going to stop for her.

HIDE, her baby said.

Stella was skeptical. Her baby lacked the kind of judgment that comes through lived experience. Then again there was something weird about the eighteen-wheeler now barreling toward her. A yellow dust shimmered from the asphalt and it made the truck look like it was hovering. At the last minute Stella jumped and crouched in a drainage ditch and hid.

The truck passed by.

Stella stood up.

She dusted herself off.

"I don't think you're really talking to me," Stella said to the baby, because she was angry, and also because her plan to hitchhike across the state to meet a man who had probably forgotten all about her was just now hitting her as unwise. "The reality is, I'm just talking to myself."

Her baby snorted.

I TRIED TO WARN YOU. OUR ENEMIES WILL TRY TO DEFEAT US. YOU SHOULDN'T HAVE STOPPED AT DENNY'S. THE FOOD WAS GREASY AND YOU COULD HAVE SPARED ME THE SUGAR HIGH FROM ALL THAT WHIPPED CREAM—

"To heck with your conspiracy theories," Stella said. "I love you, baby, but you have some funny ideas about the world."

Time passed, a lot of it.

No one stopped to give her a ride.

Stella's continuing efforts to look worthy, while one car after another rushed by without stopping for her, left her feeling glum. Also she was hungry. Also she needed to pee. She began to wonder how risky it would be to walk over to the Texaco station across the way. She could

use the bathroom, and she could buy some food at the Mini-Mart. But maybe she would miss a ride. She didn't know what to do. The sun hung as flat as a cheap wafer behind a haze of yellow clouds. A no-wind, heavy-air feeling came over her, weighing her down and making her shoulders slump. As the hours passed she couldn't help but dwell on the facts. She was a pregnant girl with many three-letter mental diagnoses and with no prospects of a good life and her baby would eventually join a gang.

Finally she said to heck with it and walked over to the Texaco station in spite of her baby's kicks of protest.

When she got there she used the restroom and it was good.

She went next to the Mini-Mart and picked out two cans of Raspberry Tea and a package of Hostess Donettes. She drank one can of Raspberry Tea while standing in line and paid for it and everything else when she got to the register. The girl who was working behind the counter was from Pakistan or Brazil. She had big dark eyes and brown skin, and softly flowing black hair that went halfway down her back. Stella thought she was beautiful.

"I've been watching you standing out there trying to get a ride," the girl behind the counter said. "Here's your change."

"Thanks," Stella said.

A television was on behind the counter. The bottom of the screen showed the Powerball numbers and the rest of the screen was filled with a man who was very agitated about something or another. His voice rose and fell. Stella lingered, because she was lonely.

READ YOUR BIBLE, MEN, the man shouted from the television. WE ARE IN THE TIME OF THE SEVENTH PLAGUE. OUR WOMEN HAVE BEEN INFECTED BY IT. YOU HAVE SEEN IT IN THEIR EYES. YOU HAVE WITNESSED THEIR DESCENT INTO BESTIAL CARNALITY.

"Wow, that guy has a way with words," Stella said, to break the ice.

"Yeah," the girl said. "There's nothing else on."

A man came in who wanted to play a thousand dollars' worth of two-dollar Powerball. Another one wanted to fill up many gasoline cans. A third one wanted to buy every six-pack and every Marlboro in the store. The girl behind the counter got too busy to talk.

Stella walked back over to her familiar patch on the shoulder of the road. She drank her second can of Raspberry Tea. She decided to save the Hostess Donettes for later. She waited in the shimmering heat until nothing seemed the way it was. The baby was sulking, or maybe gloating over her suffering. She began to cry. She would be sleeping in a ditch that night. There was no traffic at all on the road. All day long there had been a rush of cars speeding northward, ignoring her, treating her like the cast-off, discarded, pregnant girl that she was, and now there was no one left to give her a ride. The road was so empty that a flock of pigeons decided to land in the middle and to pick at the grit.

"At least you could keep me company," Stella said, to the baby. "Hold up your end of the conversation, that is."

Before the baby could answer a beautiful brown girl with softly flowing black hair—the very same one who had been working at the Texaco Mini-Mart—drove by and then pulled over on the shoulder and honked.

Stella ran over.

"I'm not going far," the girl said. "Only about seven miles."

"Okay," Stella said, and got in.

They started off. Stella felt shy and grateful.

"Where are you going?" the girl said.

Stella told her.

"That's pretty far. Maybe five, six hours from here."

After a few miles the girl said, "You can stay with us tonight I bet. I live with my foster parents. I'll tell them you're a friend. It's going to get dark soon. You're really pregnant. I can tell them that your parents kicked you out. Did they? My foster parents like to help kids in need."

"Your foster parents wouldn't call anybody? The police?"

The girl shook her head.

"They understand about police," she said. "My name is Basheera. You can call me Bibi. This is my foster mom's car. She lets me drive it to work because the bus schedule around here is non-existent."

The girl's voice was earnest and enthusiastic in the way of helpful people.

"I bet you're hungry," Bibi said. "My foster mom is not a good cook. She makes mac-and-cheese every night. My foster mom is deaf in one ear. Just now she takes care of me and she takes care of two little meth babies. They were born that way, addicted to meth. My foster mom takes the kids that other foster parents won't take. All the time the agency is calling her up and saying, 'Edith, oh, Edith, can't you take just one more?' She'll probably ask you to stay for as long as you want. You're like a two-for-one deal. My foster dad is a carpenter. He's in the union. This is it. This is where we get off the highway."

Chapter Eleven
Wanda Lubiejewski's Daughter Grows Up

All that day Wanda Lubiejewski found herself running through a bilious fragrant yellow haze while cradling her daughter in her mighty jaws. Now and then her daughter would open her eyes and then close them again. Wanda Lubiejewski heard cars honking and sirens screaming all around her, following her wherever she ran. Sometimes people took her picture with their phones before scuttling off into their houses and closing all the doors and windows behind them. Some of them wore gas masks. Others held hankies over their noses. Others stumbled about like animals with incoherent looks on their faces, and wept. The roads were packed with cars and animals of every kind. She cradled her daughter in her jaws as gently as she could under the circumstances. The girl had lost consciousness but beyond a certain limpness her daughter was no worse for wear.

As Wanda Lubiejewski ran she was intensely aware of the way her muscles clenched and relaxed and clenched again beneath her loose and luxuriant fur. It was marvelous, the way she could run, for miles and miles, without ever having that familiar feeling of her bra straps digging into her shoulders, or the feeling of her breasts slapping her ribcage like wet sand bags with each step. She was no longer sure she had breasts at all, beneath the fur. The idea exhilarated her. Although she could not have described in words what she was running toward, her muscles seemed to know, and that knowledge made her body feel exultant and purposeful. She noticed that she was instinctively running away from paved places. She ran up a hill and past a wind farm and then down the other side, where she found herself running along a riverbank, a habitat full of oak and eucalyptus trees that afforded her camouflage.

Preoccupied by the feeling of her muscular thick body in motion, she ran straight into an encampment of three men, by the river. The men ran away shouting.

They left behind a pleasant fire.

Wanda Lubiejewski put her girl down. She felt proud of her girl that she could play "dead" so expertly. Then she fretted that the three men who had run off would soon come back to their encampment, and maybe bring guns with them. But ever since her metamorphosis her sense of smell had grown ever more discerning, and she was beginning to realize that she could trust her instincts. There would be plenty of warning if those pungent men did decide to come back. Just by raising her head to catch the wind she could tell that the men were running away from her at top speed, and the closest other humans were miles away. She could smell the overpowering diesel and gasoline from the nearest road, four miles to the east. She could smell the spoor of the men around the camp. An understanding of the living things surrounding her on all sides presented itself in her mind like a map, just from breathing in. She could smell scat that traced the routes of skunk and vole and gopher and deer through these woods. She could smell the ants as they made their tunnels beneath her. She could smell the yellow jackets in their nest in the roots of a tan oak tree, three miles away.

The men had left behind a bag of groceries, spilled on the ground.

A broken bottle of hard apple cider sinking into the ground.

A loaf of bread.

A bunch of bananas.

Her girl loved bananas.

Wanda Lubiejewski picked the bananas up and peeled one of them with her big lips and placed it on the ground in front of her child. The girl rose out of her stupor and her eyes flickered open. Wanda tried to look small and without malice. Her girl had stopped crying at least, and instead she looked merely exhausted and resigned to be eaten.

Wanda tried to speak to her girl, but the same harsh, hard, resonant grumbles came out of her as when she had tried to speak to her husband, long ago, back at the house just before her husband had tried to shoot her. She soon discovered that she could modulate her pitch a little, though, and before long she managed to hum—in an unfamiliar, low bass-baritone, to be sure—a passable version of her daughter's favorite lullaby.

"Go to sleep my baby, close your big brown eyes," she hummed.

"Are you a magic bear?" the girl whispered. Wanda nodded her vast and ragged head. She nudged a banana closer with her snout and her girl began to eat. After she was done eating the girl brought a book out from under her shirt that she had somehow managed to carry along with her. She held it up to the bear. Wanda recognized it as the one she had read to her daughter every night for the last eleven months. "You're in my book!" her daughter said. The girl settled in between her mother's huge front paws and began to read.

On they flee through yellow fog—
A pregnant girl, a talking dog—
And soon they meet a magic bear
Who gives them food, and combs their hair.

Her girl droned on in her sweet little voice. Wanda Lubiejewski's thoughts began to wander. It had been a stressful time for her, truth be told, and the stress had taken its toll. She was exhausted. She must have fallen asleep, because the next thing she knew she woke with a start, alerted by a sharp-sweet smell rising up from the skin of her little girl, her beloved daughter, who had let the book drop on the ground and was trembling. Although the girl was not afraid of her mother any longer, her scent was full of a new fear, brought on by changes that were beginning to make themselves known in the girl's body.

There was no doubt about it. Her daughter's body was beginning to mature. Already she had sprouted the beginnings of fur between her legs, and her torso was becoming thick and strong, and her jaws and snout were evolving, too. Soon the small-girl body would become something wild and animal. Wanda remembered the terror of her own transformation. She licked the girl's face. She breathed out a blanket of soft deep warmth over the child's body. She hummed her low hums and thought: "how heartbreaking it is, to be a mother, and to love so much, and to not be able to shield a child from all the things that must be endured while growing up."

But children are more adaptable than their parents can ever know or remember. Unlike her mother, the girl changed quickly, within minutes. Soon the girl was sleek and black-furred and fiercely adolescent and she stood nearly as high as her mother, each of them over twelve feet tall from paw to shoulder even when on all fours, and twice as tall when standing on their back legs.

"Roar," the girl said.

Chapter Twelve
A Prayer of Thanksgiving

The beautiful Bibi drove with Stella past fields full of rusted frames of trucks, past streets of blocky houses painted in shades of pink and yellow and orange, and past some fenced-in patches of dirt and weeds. Out the window Stella saw many dogs and donkeys, and an alpaca or two, and some cows, but strangely no people at all. No other cars, either. It felt as if every person in the world had decided to run away that very afternoon. Bibi turned left and drove to the end of a road, to a house that

might have been the original farmhouse in those parts before the subdivisions happened. The house looked ready to fall down. Both of Bibi's foster parents were in the kitchen. The foster dad was drinking something from a paper bag. The foster mom was heating bottles of milk on the stove. The two meth babies were laid out on their backs in a white-mesh playpen in the corner. They sucked on their little fingers and kicked their legs.

Looking down at those little meth babies in their playpen, Stella thought more concretely than ever before about the reality of her own baby, a baby who would eventually be born, and who would eventually become something like these babies lying in the white-mesh playpen. Stella thought: "Will my baby still speak in complete sentences after birth, too? How weird is that?" She stared at the meth babies and tried to imagine becoming a mother. Stella was not addicted to meth, of course, and so her baby would not be a meth baby, but still these meth babies were babies, just like her baby would be a baby one day.

I AM NOTHING LIKE THOSE METH BABIES, her baby said, and kicked her a little. EGO SUM ET ANTICHRISTUS. EGO SUM DOMINUS PESTIFER MUNDI

There was a moist, sweet-heavy scent of diaper in the air.

There were three hounds drooling and sleeping under the kitchen table.

There was a plastic clock in the shape of an owl on the wall and its eyes moved left, right, left, in time with the clock's plastic pendulum.

A mound of dirty dishes filled the sink and spilled over.

"Well hi there, Bibi," the foster mom said. "Who's your little friend?"

"Stella. She needs a place to stay. Can she?"

"Well of course she can," the foster mom said.

The foster mom dried her hands on a dishtowel and stepped forward and held her hand out and Stella shook it.

"Hello there, Stella," the foster mom said.

"Hello there, Stella," the foster dad echoed placidly. "Come have a seat here at the table if you like."

"We're just going up to my room," Bibi said. "I want to show Stella some stuff."

"All right," the foster dad said. He spoke in a tone that reminded Stella of old TV shows with fathers in them.

"Dinner is in fifteen minutes I guess," said the foster mom.

"Yeah, okay," Bibi said.

Stella followed Bibi up a flight of stairs. Some places on the wall were just bare wood. The stairs had a mix of rug and bare floorboard. At the top of the stairs Bibi opened a door and they went in. Inside was a tidy room and the twin beds were made neatly. Bibi sat on one of the beds and then stretched out on it like a long sleek cat.

"Is this your room?" Stella said.

"Yeah. I used to share it with a girl named Lois Latsky. She ran away. Now I have the room to myself."

"Oh."

Stella sat down on Lois Latsky's former bed and bounced a little.

"It's a nice room," Stella said.

She could tell they liked each other. For some reason it felt like secret knowledge and maybe even a little embarrassing.

Bibi stared at her.

"So why are you having this baby, anyway?" Bibi said.

Stella's face felt hot. It hadn't been her plan to get pregnant. But something had compelled her. Now that she thought about it, she knew why.

"This baby is special," she said. "This baby is going to change the world."

Bibi looked at her. The look wasn't mean. She didn't say "you are mentally ill," or "that's stupid, don't you know every pregnant girl wants to believe her kid is special," or, "what makes you, a nobody, think you'll somehow have a baby that matters," or any of the other things that anyone other than Bibi might have said.

"Okay," Bibi said.

Bibi stretched out an arm and turned on a plastic pink radio by the bed.

THE GOVERNMENT IS USING CELL TOWER SIGNALS TO TURN THE AMERICAN PEOPLE INTO COMPLACENT ANIMALS, the man on the radio said. THEN THE GOVERNMENT TAKES THEM AWAY TO THE SLAUGHTER. THIS IS HAPPENING TO YOUR NEIGHBORS. THIS IS NO METAPHOR, PEOPLE. THIS IS TRUE. THIS IS HAPPENING RIGHT NOW. IT'S THE LITERAL END OF THE WORLD MY FRIENDS

"Wow, there they go again," Bibi said.

She tried to find another station and then made a sound and turned the radio off.

"You can't believe anything you hear anymore," Stella said.

"Nothing's good anymore," Bibi said.

"You're good," Stella said.

"You're good, too," Bibi said.

Bibi got up and walked over to the door and locked it and walked back to her bed and sat down again. They looked at one another. Then out of courtesy they looked away. Stella trained her eye on several objects in the room, one after another, and feigned to study them with interest. A chair. A stuffed animal. A lamp in the corner. Stella's breathing was low and shallow and her heart hurt a little bit. Also she was ravenous. She remembered the Hostess Donettes in her L.L. Bean tote bag, the same Hostess Donettes she had bought from Bibi a few hours earlier. She felt overwhelmed by the sense that she and Bibi had known one another for such a long time.

"Do you ever wonder what the heck is going on in the world?" Bibi said.

Stella thought about it.

"No, not really," she said.

"Dinner!" the foster mom shouted, from below.

Dinner that night wasn't mac-and-cheese at all. It was Hamburger Helper on top of Wonder Bread. Stella discovered that this family was the kind of family where the adults compelled everyone at the table to clasp hands together and pray thanks over the meal.

"We praise Thee, Lord," the foster dad said. "You are the One who sets up kings and topples empires. We thank Thee for letting us be born in these United States. We thank Thee for sending the little lost Black girl Stella to break bread with us. Amen!"

When the foster dad prayed, instead of sounding like a TV dad, he sounded like a TV preacher. Stella found the change in his voice and facial expression remarkable. Her baby was kicking so hard Stella could hardly sit without yelling. After the foster dad was done with his prayer he let go of Stella's hand and the baby settled down.

They began to eat.

Something like thunder or maybe bombs going off in the distance made the room vibrate. No one mentioned it. Not even the meth babies seemed bothered. Stella wanted to ask about the bombs, or whatever they were, but the foster dad started talking first.

"What's a young Black girl like you doing out on her own?" the foster dad said.

"I like being alone," Stella said.

"Ridiculous," the foster dad said. "Women and girls are useless on their own. They're weak. Right, honey?"

"Right, honey," the foster mom said.

"Exactly," the foster dad said. "A man on his own can accomplish things. Look at Samson. Look at Jesus. Look at God. Women are a different story. You women need to gather together. You can't do anything on your own. That's why you have those knitting circles. And bake sales."

"And book clubs," the foster mom said.

"Ha, ha," the foster dad said.

"Anyway I'm not alone," Stella said. She was thinking of her baby.

"That's right," the foster mom said. "You're perfectly right. None of us is ever truly alone when we walk with the Lord."

A low rumble came rolling on through the kitchen, and the table shook, and the windows rattled in their frames, and the spigot over the sink started to run on its own.

The foster mom got up and cranked the spigot hard and it stopped.

"Tell me, Stella," said the foster dad. "Do you walk with the Lord? Would it be all right if we pray for you and your baby? May we?"

The foster mom and foster dad looked at her with joyous expectation while Bibi scooped up some Hamburger Helper on a spoon and ate it.

To tell the truth, Stella was reluctant to be prayed over. From what she'd seen of religion it mainly seemed to be a way to make people believe that they deserved their troubles.

And it bothered her that God only granted special favors if you prayed to Him.

And come to think of it God's need for constant, fawning attention seemed a little immature on God's part, especially for Somebody supposedly all-powerful and so on.

And if that weren't enough, it also seemed true that, when it came to religion, girls were always getting the short end.

But Stella was a guest, and she knew her manners.

"Okay," she said.

Shockingly—she was not expecting it to go that far—the foster mom laid her hands on Stella's belly with vigor. So did the foster dad, and he even pushed his wife's hands a little to one side so he could get a good grip.

Bibi shyly put one hand on Stella's shoulder.

"Heavenly Father," the foster dad said.

ITA GENIUM AD INFEROS! THE SOW IS MINE! her baby yelled.

"Stop that, stop it!" Stella shouted, and covered her ears.

The foster parents wrenched their hands away from Stella's pregnant belly like it was on fire.

Stella began to wonder about her baby's origins.

"What are you and what do you want?" she gasped.

EGO SUM DOMINUS PESTIFER MUNDI, the baby reminded her.

"We're people of God," the foster dad said. "We don't want anything. We've heard God's call and have answered him with open and contrite hearts."

"Well, okay," Stella said. "But I don't think I've heard the call just yet myself."

"With God's mercy one day you will," the foster dad said. He sounded disgruntled.

"I'm sorry," Stella said. "I'm sure one day I will."

They all quickly turned their attention to the food on their plates. They ate like they wished everyone else would leave the table. Nobody said anything. Stella's ears were ringing. Her baby seemed to have gone into a deep retreat. The foster dad nurtured himself by putting bits of Hamburger Helper on his finger and then dangling his hand under the table so the dogs could take turns licking it off of his fingertip. The foster mom picked up the meth babies from their playpen and kissed the tops of their heads and sniffed their scalps, exactly as if those little scalps were the sweetest smell in the world. Then she sat down at the table with both meth babies in her lap, and with their bottles propped up on a pillow as they nursed, and she tried to eat her own meal at the same time, even though it was impossible.

Every once in a while Bibi would look up and catch Stella's eye and smile and Stella would feel better.

After dinner Bibi and Stella washed the dishes together while the foster parents went to the next room and watched the TV News with the meth babies in their laps. Bibi and Stella could hear the familiar voice of the President through the open door, especially because the foster parents turned the volume up on account of the foster mom's one deaf ear.

WE WILL MAKE AMERICA SAFE AGAIN. BELIEVE ME. THE AMERICAN PEOPLE HAVE ENDURED ONE BRUTAL ATTACK AFTER ANOTHER. CHILDREN SLAUGHTERED. GIRLS CARRIED OFF IN THE SLAVERING JAWS OF BEASTS. WOMEN HUNTED DOWN BY THESE ANIMALS.

Bibi's right hand and Stella's left hand touched now and then in the soapy water.

"My foster parents seemed weird to me at first, too," Bibi said. "But I got used to it. I was raised in a different religion altogether."

"Oh."

"Do you want to watch television after we're done here?"

"Not really," Stella said.

"Tired?"

"Yeah."

When the dishes were done they went back upstairs.

Bibi tried the radio again.

AMERICAN CARNAGE—

Bibi turned it off. Stella asked if she could take a shower and Bibi showed her where the shower was and gave her a towel. When Stella got back from her shower Bibi was already in bed. Stella got in the same bed, next to Bibi, not really meaning it, more like they were both pretending to mean it.

"I never kissed a girl before," Stella said.

"I never kissed a pregnant girl before," Bibi said.

Bibi put her hand on Stella's knee. It was a kind of question. Bibi's hand was cold and Stella laughed because it tickled. They kissed. Bibi slid her hand between Stella's legs. Stella laughed again and took Bibi's hand away from there and put it on her big belly instead.

"Do you think I'm bad?" Bibi said.

"No, you're good," Stella said. "We're both good, remember?"

"You're so round," Bibi said. "You look like you swallowed a basketball."

"Yeah, that's how it happened," Stella said.

They kissed some more. And then, ever so slowly, they began to introduce one another to an idyllic garden filled with earthly delights, and with skanky delights, too; and the baby thank goodness slept through it, and the two girls didn't stop until they traveled absolutely everywhere together, inside and out, and when they were done they slept in each other's arms, perfectly content.

Book Three

Signals and Signs

ARTIST'S RENDERING: "AGENT-T"

CENTER FOR DISEASE CONTROL (CDC)

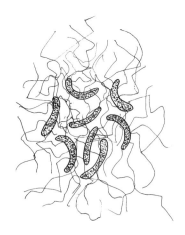

Chapter Thirteen
Major Eureka Yamanaka Ponders Acts of God

Major Eureka Yamanaka had long ago learned for the sake of her career to hide her intelligence behind large thick glasses and everyone usually ignored her because of it. No one really noticed her or bothered to give her new orders these days. They all thought someone else was in charge of her. She wasn't happy to be confined in the underground nuclear Command Center with a nuclear football, the most useless thing possible to be in charge of while stationed in the most advanced and most secure and most lethal nuclear launch site ever built. But it seemed prudent to wait quietly for her next orders rather than to go out looking for trouble.

From the scattered news feeds still coming from the surface she began to think that insurance companies would soon be in for a beating. Drones flying over the country just that morning sent back pictures of one unlikely event after another. A pack of dingoes sniffed their way down Wilshire Boulevard in Los Angeles. A buffalo herd, three miles across, thundered north along the Maine coastline. A solitary white rhino ran through a district of downtown San Diego. Giant bears roamed at will on the Washington Mall, snuffing at the monuments and attacking anyone on sight who came near. Rumors were rampant: that the country had been hit by a terrorist attack; that Big Pharma had released a toxin to make a profit on the antidote; that genetically modified foods had corrupted human DNA; that the Vice President had declared himself President; that the Vice President had turned into a Bichon Frisé.

But then again, sometimes the view from the feeds looked so normal that Major Eureka Yamanaka fell back into believing what most of them believed, here underground: that they were victims of foreign propaganda, and nothing more.

She watched a feed from a drone flying across the heartland. The soldier piloting the drone trained the camera on a man harrowing clods of dirt on his tractor, half-asleep as he rode.

She watched a boy on a trampoline just north of Flint, Michigan, as he graced a different drone with a perfect back flip.

She saw pick-up basketball games and potlucks in county parks.

She imagined that these scenes of normal people leading normal lives were a made-up story, to keep the people from panicking.

Then she reversed her thinking and became convinced that Agent-T was the made-up story, pushed by the country's enemies to paralyze the President here underground, while the real world went on as usual with its simple pleasures.

She couldn't make up her mind which was the real America, and which was the fake one.

That day the President woke at noon. He complained about the coffee. He read a speech in front of many flags. He wanted to bust right out of this concrete bunker and fly off to somewhere more scenic. A golf course, maybe. To distract him his Chief of Staff suggested a series of precision air strikes along the border of Mexico, plus a few other targets besides, like Fresno and Los Angeles, or Korea and Burkina Faso.

"Nuclear?" said the President.

"Maybe not today," said a ranking general.

"Well, I don't want to take cards off the table," said the President. "The last person to press that button would be me. The last person that wants to play the nuclear card, believe me, is me. But you can never take cards off the table either from a moral standpoint and certainly from a negotiating standpoint."

The Generals all agreed that you could never take the cards off the table.

"But then again maybe not today," Major Eureka Yamanaka said.

They all looked at her.

The President squinted.

"Quite cheeky, but I like your pretty smile," the President said. "Say your say, Captain."

"You should order something more tactical, maybe, sir," Major Eureka Yamanaka said. "So you leave some cards on the table."

The President thought about it.

"Brilliant," he said. "I hereby give the order for something more tactical. So we leave some cards on the table. Get going, men."

Soon they were all in the command room watching the paths of five tactical missiles make merry arcs across the screens. When the missiles landed, up from each impact came a cloud of yellow dust. The Generals cheered and slapped one another's backs and shook hands heartily. And the wind carried the yellow dust north, where it rose into the troposphere, and then it flowed toward the pole, and then it doubled back toward the equator, and passed over the equator, to repeat the pattern in the southern hemisphere, mixing and flowing, until all the world was blanketed by softly falling, flowing, sullen-yellow molecules; and one plume of the stuff settled on the Mountain covering the underground Command Center, where it brooded over the bent world and made its way seepingly inside.

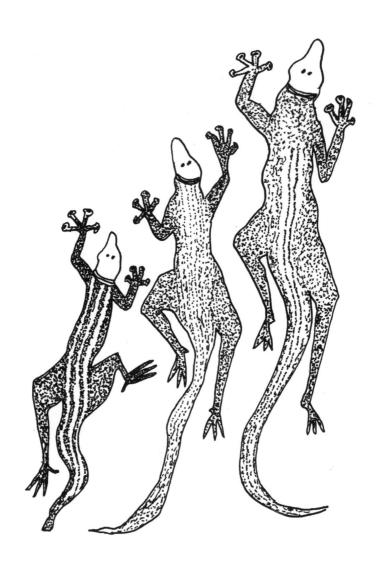

Chapter Fourteen

Mary Mbwembwe Meets Margie Peach and Does Not Know Her

As for Mary Mbwembwe, it got darker and darker that night until she finally pulled off at the next rest stop and cut the engine and began to cry because she realized she didn't know anything at all about where she was going, and she was an undocumented worker in her forties with no family, no health care, and no friends, and incidentally she had a big knot in her neck from driving too long without a break.

Also she was a bad person: how could she even think of leaving the old woman in the hands of a daughter who visited her mother just once a year, at Christmas? When the daughter did visit she just sat in a chair next to the bed and yelled at her mother, as if there were still so many old scores to settle, while the old woman lay in bed with a gentle smile on her powdered face. Mary Mbwembwe had not loved the old woman. Even so, to think that there would be no one at the funeral who had witnessed the old woman's monumental heroic daily struggles to maintain her dignity in the face of one indignity after another—the rectal incontinence, the crumbling teeth, the skin on her forearms that ripped and bruised at the slightest touch (though never bedsores—Mary Mbwembwe had made sure of that)—made Mary Mbwembwe feel as if everything was wrong in the world.

She got out of the car and slammed the door.

She found herself standing alone and in the dark, with no one to pity her.

A line of big trucks was laid out in a row at one end of the parking lot. They looked like hulking monuments. She couldn't see anyone in them.

In fact there weren't any people anywhere.

It was exactly as if the people had parked those trucks and had walked away into the darkness forever.

Two cinder-block buildings were lit by bare bulbs and the bulbs were covered in a fog of moths.

There were no cars on the road.

No sound of human conversation.

Mary Mbwembwe shivered. She could have been, at that moment, the only person left in the world.

She looked up and saw the moon was still there, same as always, and it comforted her.

Only she could not help but notice that there was a strange smoke hovering in the air, a yellow haze that made the moon look veiled. The air smelled equally of disinfectant and moldering organic matter, almost as if she were still back in the old woman's house and had never left it.

Cows lowed in the distance.

Mary Mbwembwe, lonely, walked toward the sound.

Within a few yards she came to a barbed wire fence, and stopped.

The cows fell silent.

A sudden hush came down on the land exactly as if the covers had been pulled up.

The sound of Mary Mbwembwe's own breathing was loud in her ears and she felt very small and afraid. If she hadn't felt so small and afraid she might not have begun just then to sing and move her feet, just a little, in the tradition of all grieving women from her home country. Her voice was soft. Then it grew stronger. She moved her feet with conviction and her tears began to flow, for the very old woman who had died alone in her bed, for herself, and for the world.

She heard something rustling toward her through the high grass of the pasture, as if called by her song.

A dog's face poked through the grass, and then the dog bounded all the way out of the grass and wagged its tail at her, as if to say, "I'm a dog, isn't it wonderful?"

But instead of saying any such thing, the dog said: "My name is Margie Peach and I breed whip-tail lizards."

It was such an unexpected conversation starter that Mary Mbwembwe ran back to her car and drove straight on until she saw a gas station lit painfully bright against the morbid dark all around it. Along with ten dollars of gas Mary Mbwembwe bought a Big Gulp, for the caffeine, and resolved to never again fall asleep behind the wheel. No one was there to take her money. So Mary Mbwembwe left some cash on the counter and drove on.

Chapter Fifteen
A Cry of Triumph

Margie Peach was an autodidact and a self-made scholar and she did not, even as a dog, rely solely on her nose to inform her about the world. She wanted to learn more about current events. She chased down every scrap of newsprint blowing through a field, or scuttering down a sidewalk, to see if she could corroborate Dr. Alberta Chen's story. Sadly though the news she came across while running about and sniffing for it was scant and suspiciously hysterical, more like tabloid news than serious journalism.

She read that California had been quarantined.

The President was bunkered deep inside an underground Command Center in Colorado.

The President had ordered tactical air strikes against Los Angeles and Fresno and Mexico and Korea and Burkina Faso.

Seven armies were on the march across Byzantium.

Ten thousand souls were missing and presumed dead following an earthquake in Lisbon.

The Euphrates had mysteriously run dry.

The citizens of Paris had disappeared overnight.

From a scrap of the *Sacramento Bee* that Margie Peach caught in her teeth she read a cockamamie story about giant bears attacking Washington. The National Guard had cornered the bears in the Capitol Rotunda and were closing in on them when without warning the troops dropped their weapons and galloped off on all fours, leaving the bears free to escape and do their worst.

The pictures looked doctored.

In a pile of trash that had blown up against a fence she found a page ripped from a child's book, and read

The girl is friendless, and with child.
The land is burnt. The road is wild.
She finds the Land of Yellow Fog
And there she meets a talking dog.

The poem seemed significant to Margie Peach, even if it was written in naïve iambs, and she tried to imagine what it could mean.

The wind changed and she lost interest in the poem and loped toward a scent she could not yet identify. She came upon a pod of sleeping cows and they started up with their dumb frantic lowing but they were not the source of the scent. Margie Peach ignored them. Now that she had become self-aware she was bored by cows rather than needing to succumb at once to her purely animal love of the hunt. She traveled on through the high grass, mindful of foxtails.

That was when she heard a beautiful sad song. She yearned for the sound. She ran toward it expectantly—all the while chastising herself for her slavish interest in finding a human companion to love her and shower her with kibble. She reached the end of the tall grass abruptly and burst out onto a patch of dirt, where she found herself face to face with a singing, swaying woman, who was dancing in the dark, all alone, at an Interstate rest stop. The woman was wearing an ankle-length skirt, and there was a long white cloth wrapped around her head, turban-like, and her song was so sad that Margie Peach began to make a mournful primitive sound of her own. Her blood and muscle flowed with the knowledge of the ages, and it felt exactly as if she understood everything at once: the end and the beginning; the past and the future; the body and the spirit.

But now the woman had stopped singing and stood rigidly, as if steeling herself for attack. Margie Peach wondered if she were in fact a fierce-looking dog, a creature that could strike fear in others if she weren't careful. Wanting to correct any false impression of hostility she began to introduce herself as she would have to any new acquaintance.

"My name is Margie Peach and I breed whip-tail lizards," she said.

The woman ran away.

Never mind, Margie thought, because she had discovered something new about herself: that she could speak not only to other dogs, but also to other humans. She resolved though to use this skill only sparingly, as no doubt it would cause terror if she revealed her skill to the wrong sorts of people, or it could lead to her being exploited by small-minded folk out to make a quick buck on reality television or another debased venue like it.

She traveled on, more thoughtful than before. The next thing Margie Peach knew she was trotting through the side yards of houses and between suburban fences. It was dark. In this part of the world the smell of Agent-T had faded to the most subtle top note and it felt as if she were back in the old world again, in the world as it had been just hours ago, when she'd been merrily on her way to drink a Cherry Coke at the Top of the Mark. The people she could smell behind the doors and in their houses were content with their routines. They put out no scent of fear. No doubt, like Margie, they had read the same hysterical news reports, and no doubt, like Margie, they had dismissed these reports as foolish puddle-dee-doo—who would ever believe such nonsense?—and she felt smug to think that she, too, had not been fooled.

While crossing a driveway she knocked over a garbage can and she stopped to sniff the bouquet. A man came out on his front step. He called out to her. He spoke soothingly. He had something in his hand: an offering. She was moving toward the most delicious smell imaginable, when snap, he snapped a collar and leash on her, and he locked her in his bland suburban back yard, with fences all around.

Now that she was stuck in a bland suburban back yard, Margie Peach had time once more to contemplate this feeling, this strangely pleasant, completely natural feeling, of living inside the body of a dog. She recalled all the times that men had called her a dog. Instead of feeling bad about it now, she wondered instead whether those men had not led her to the truth. Granted, she was still getting used to being a dog. About half the time she was still her old self, Margie Peach, a woman who happened to find herself inside the body of a dog. The other half of the time—maybe more than half—she was completely a dog, through and through, living moment to moment, joyously tugging hard enough to rid herself of collar and chain; joyously digging a hole under the fence, her nose encrusted in glorious dirt, and how strong her front paws were, how strong she felt! And she was halfway to freedom when Animal Control showed up and stuck her in a box and loaded her into the back of a service van.

"I need to contemplate my current reality," she told herself sternly, from inside the box. "I need to understand it, and find a way out of it."

She tried to think. At first the only thought she could manage was a brooding sense that she did not like the box in which she found herself. Then more metaphysical questions occurred to her. What about life expectancy? What was her age in dog-years? What if she were hallucinating? What if she were dead? What if this was the end of the world?

Something was biting her right paw, a flea.

She bit back in a furious tooth-bared assault and felt better.

The door of the service van opened and the man carried her box—with difficulty; she was not a small dog—into a building full of barks and yips, and also full of the overwhelming scent of Pine Sol, which made the inside of her nose sting and her eyes water.

Next she found herself locked in a kennel with a concrete floor that smelled of the piss of its former, terrified occupant.

They left a bowl of pernicious food in the corner and went away.

She began to whine, the saddest most pathetic sound a dog can make.

She thought: "is this the way the world ends, not with a bang, but a whimper?" and fell into a funk.

Newspapers lined her cage.

She yelped in delight and looked closer. Her double vision still plagued her. Or maybe it was just the way dogs always saw things up close. The headlines were the easiest to read and she read these first.

THIRTY-THREE THOUSAND MISSING
EYEWITNESS ACCOUNTS OF THE RAPTURE
THE PRESIDENT DECLARES WAR ON ALL NATIONS

She stepped carefully around her kennel, taking care to not rip the paper with her claws, looking for more reasonable stories. Much to her disgust the floor of the kennel was covered with ridiculous nonsense, verging on propaganda. She read about police rescuing young children from a place that was a pizzeria by day and a pedophilia ring by night. She read about a ship off the coast of San Diego that had run aground, its crew gone and its decks overrun with exotic animals. She read about people flying up into the air, defying gravity and disappearing in the presumed direction of Heaven. Cherubim sightings were on the rise. Ports along the entire circumference of the Mediterranean were overgrown with an unknown fungal invasive species. Mt. Fuji had erupted. Hong Kong had sunk without a trace. The polar ice cap was missing. Mass suicides. Internment camps. Dirty bombs. She peed on the last story and put the so-called news straight out of her head and began to plan her escape. After the people turned out the lights and went home, Margie Peach got to work at liberating herself. Fortunately her kennel had not been built to hold problem-solving kinds of creatures. There was no lock on the door of her cage. There was only a latch. Not that it was a piece of cake to get

the latch undone, given that her hands, or her paws rather, no longer clasped things easily. But after many tries she was able to unlatch the door and step out. The other dogs howled for their own release. Why not? One by one Margie Peach gave them their freedom.

The front door of the shelter was bolted and she could not open it. Margie Peach explored her options. The other dogs followed her wherever she went, pretending to search the building with her and wagging their tails with stupid pride, as if they were, by wagging, helping her find a way out for them all. The first few hallways all ended in windows with bars across them. Finally she padded down a darkened corridor where she discovered the emergency exit door. Even though she could read the warning, and even though she knew an alarm would sound, it was the only way out.

Margie Peach pushed on the door with her front feet and it opened out into the night. The alarm when it sounded was like a cry of triumph. Margie Peach ran. The other dogs followed her. She was running with a pack and it exhilarated her, especially now that she knew where she was going. In her mind Margie saw the pregnant girl, and she remembered the girl's scent, and then somehow she caught that scent on the wind, as it rose above the diesel exhaust and the pizza crusts and the beer bottles and the pesticides and the baked-tar asphalt roads, still warm from the day.

And Margie Peach followed Stella's scent north, and west, and the other dogs followed Margie.

Chapter Sixteen
Josefina Guzman Watches 'Noticiero Telemundo'

Josefina Guzman began to notice that the world around her had gone dead silent.

No more crying of birds and sea lions. No stirring of wind in the reeds. No chirrup of insects or echo of traffic from a distant highway.

The only thing that disturbed the silence was the whine of a military drone that hovered above her until she shook her fishing pole at it and it flew away.

But then she felt uneasy in the silence that the drone left behind. She decided that before it was fully dark she would walk the dirt path to the village. She could maybe watch Noticiero Telemundo with Father Juan del Rosario and others of the parish who were interested in keeping up with the daily news. She set off, pacing herself. When she got to the rectory she knocked on the door. A little girl she did not recognize opened it and then ran back through the hall without saying a hello or wipe-your-shoes. Josefina Guzman found her own way down the hall, to the room where Father Juan del Rosario and some parishioners were crowded around the TV set. A boy got up and gave Josefina Guzman his place by the stove. She sat down. The general feeling in the room was one of hysterical frivolity approaching panic. Josefina Guzman noted it.

"Josefina Guzman, I am so glad you are here," Father Juan del Rosario said. "Look, look, look at this. Watch! Some of us are claiming that Noticiero Telemundo tonight is the same Noticiero Telemundo as it was last night!"

"It used to just sound like the same old news every day," said a woman in front, "but now it is the same news exactly."

"Yesterday's news is being played again today?" Father Juan Del Rosario said. "How can that be?"

It sounded to Josefina Guzman as if they were all poking fun at her. She was familiar with the way the same old stories kept playing again and again on the daily news, over the days and weeks and years. She didn't care much for teasing, though, and was of the general opinion that old people in particular should never be teased. Even so the wood stove was very good to be sitting next to. A young man brought her a cup of something warm to drink and she thanked him. Then the young man sat down on the floor in front of the set and joined the game they were all playing, of shouting out the next sentence the news announcer was about to say. Some of the young people were even pretending this very same broadcast had been aired not only yesterday but also for the whole week, exactly the same.

"Maybe there's something funny going on," said Father Juan del Rosario.

Josefina Guzman was dismayed to think that the priest had been taken in by the young people's antics.

"Watch, Father, this guy is going to say 'thirty-three thousand people have been reported missing in Los Angeles County,'" the young man said. The young man deepened his voice, to mimic the voice of the newsman.

"That's a lot of people," Father Juan del Rosario said.

"Thirty-three thousand people have been reported missing in Los Angeles County," said the man on the television. The man on the television looked as if he, too, were disgusted by the way the daily news never changed from one day to the next.

"Neat trick," Josefina Guzman said.

"No trick, look, I'll do it again," the young man said. "Now he is going to say, 'Next up footage of a white rhinoceros rampaging

through the Historic Gaslamp Quarter of San Diego.'"

The young man was exuberant in the way of young men who feel that others don't pay enough attention to them.

"Next up footage of a white rhinoceros rampaging through the Historic Gaslamp Quarter of San Diego," the newsman said.

"Well, after all, I think a white rhinoceros sighting would be a rare enough event for it to make the news two days in a row," said Father Juan del Rosario.

"No, you don't get it, it's the same video, the exact same video all week!" said the young man exuberantly. And he slapped his thigh and shook his head.

"What's the Gaslighting quarter?" somebody said. "Is it part of a zoo?"

"Has anyone been out of town lately?" Josefina Guzman said, and they all looked at her, because they were not used to her asking questions.

"My car is shot," Father Juan del Rosario said. "I need to wait until Ephraim gets back from visiting his girlfriend. He's been gone three days. I can't get any other garage to answer my call."

The people in the room looked at one another, back and forth.

"Look, you people," Josefina Guzman said. "Has no one been out of town lately? It could be the end of the world for all you know."

Truth be told none of them had been anywhere at all for the last few days. To Josefina Guzman, who had lived through more than one disaster, it looked as if they had a premonition that they would be better off not knowing what was going on in the world. People had a way of thinking that if they ignored bad news long enough it would go away.

"Anyone here have a telephone I can borrow?" Josefina Guzman said.

"Of course, Josefina Guzman," the young man said. "Everyone in the world has a telephone except you. You can use my phone if you want."

He handed her a contraption and she handed it back because she did not know how to make it work. She told him the number of her eldest son, who lived in Seattle. The young man tapped on the contraption and then he handed it to her, and she lifted the thing to her ear and waited. It rang many times, and then it stopped ringing, and Josefina Guzman heard a low humming in her ear.

She handed the phone back.

"It isn't working," she said. "I want to try my son in Fresno."

"Sure," the young man said, and when she told him the number he tapped a finger on his phone the same way as before and handed it to her. This time there was no ringing at all. The hum came right away and rose in pitch and volume like a mounting scream.

"No good," Josefina Guzman said, and handed it back.

The others had taken their own little phones out of their purses and pockets and they were tapping on the little screens and holding the phones to their ears. Josefina Guzman imagined them each hearing the same humming because they looked perplexed and they shook the phones before giving up. Then she heard the humming sound for real, not coming from a phone, but from all around, outside the rectory, above them, in the streets, in the sky.

They all went outside to see what was going on.

The sky was red and brooding and the stars pulsed.

"I'm going home," Josefina Guzman said.

"Maybe you should stay in town, Josefina Guzman," said Father Juan del Rosario. "Something odd is going on. Look at all these birds. Maybe there is going to be an earthquake or some other natural disaster. Birds are the first to know."

"I'm going home," Josefina Guzman said again.

She began to walk that way.

"Francisco will walk with you," Father Juan del Rosario said. "Go with her, Paco, go."

Josefina Guzman walked as fast as she could. The young man struggled to keep up. After a while she told the young man that she was fine, and that she could get home without his help, and good night. She could see that the boy wanted to be home himself, with his own family, and that he did not want to escort a strange old woman with feathers in her hair back to her shipping container in the reeds by the bay. The young man said good-bye respectfully, if a little quickly, and walked away in the direction of town. Now that Josefina Guzman was alone she was more nervous than she had expected to be, and her fears made the walk back home one of jitters and jumps. Every small sound alerted her to the feeling she had inside, that all was not well.

As soon as she reached her little clearing she saw her white stone glinting in the starlight, and it made her feel welcome.

Funny, though. The stone looked bigger than before. Now it looked as big as her fist.

She walked right up to the stone and stood there and looked down at it and tried to make her thoughts settle on the truth. She remembered it being a smaller stone, one that had fit in her pocket easily. Gradually she accepted the truth about the stone: it had been as big as her fist all along. She had also neglected to notice before what was so clear to her now: that there were markings etched in the stone, in what looked like an ancient script, and the markings were so bright and distinct that they seemed to be glowing in the dark. Josefina Guzman bent over to take a closer look, but it was like no language she had ever seen before, so she gave up and went to bed.

Book Four

Collapse and Confusion

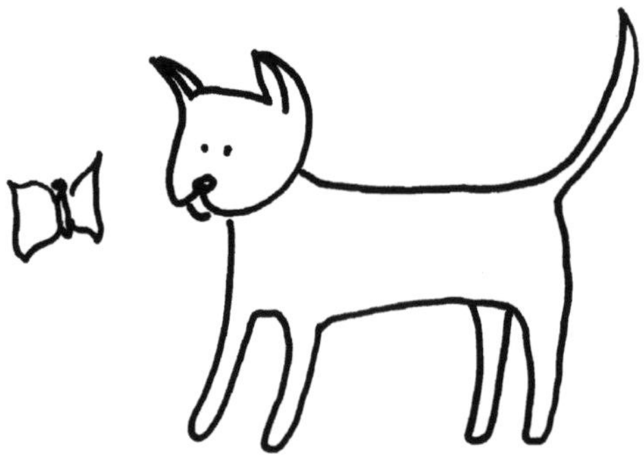

Chapter Seventeen
Stella Acquires a Pocket-Sized Pink Bible, and a Cat

Then it was morning and Stella was busy contemplating how ordinary and happy her life had become when somebody knocked on the bedroom door. When Stella hollered to come in, the foster dad opened it and presented her with a pocket-sized pink Bible for her to keep.

"Where's Bibi?" Stella asked.

"Bibi went to school. The wife took the meth babies to be checked out by a doctor. They looked like Hell this morning, pardon the expression. If you need help just say the word. I know many people. Our church sponsors runaways."

"Why thank you very much," Stella said. "But I'm not a runaway. I have family in Nethalem. They gave me money for the trip. They'll be expecting me soon. Today or tomorrow I will be reuniting with my husband."

"Well then, you just take that there Bible with you," he said. "And whenever you have a question, you just go on and open up that Bible, and the answer will appear. The Bible is a hotline to God Almighty Himself."

"This Bible?"

"That's right."

"Just open it up?"

"That's right."

She opened it as a gesture of good will and she read aloud: THE END OF ALL THINGS IS AT HAND.

"Peter-chapter-one-verse-four," the foster dad said.

"Wow, you got it," Stella said.

The foster dad looked like he was waiting for another test so Stella opened the little pink book again, and read: THE WOLF SHALL DWELL WITH THE LAMB, AND THE LEOPARD SHALL LIE DOWN WITH THE KID; AND THE CALF AND THE YOUNG LION AND THE FATLING TOGETHER; AND A LITTLE CHILD SHALL LEAD THEM.

"Isaiah-chapter-eleven-verse-six," the foster dad said. "All right, sweetie. You don't want to use all the mojo up at once. Take your time. Come on down when you're ready and I'll feed you breakfast and then I'll drive you to the bus station if you like."

The kindly foster dad went out.

For a skinny second Stella thought about how nice it would be to stay there forever with the kindly foster parents and Bibi and the two meth babies. No one would miss her. Lix Tetrax wasn't going to greet her with open arms, let's face it. If he knew she was coming he would probably get on his Harley Soft Tail Fat Boy pronto and ride away. On the other hand when she tried to imagine staying with the foster family a feeling of itchy urgency came over her, and she remembered her plan, and knew she had to get Nethalem no matter what.

That's when a big brown cat with white mitts came out from under the bed and jumped on the bed and looked at her, the way cats do. It began to knead her pregnant belly and to hum. Stella scratched it under the chin.

After a while she pushed the cat away and got up and went to the bathroom and washed up. She changed her shirt and underwear. When she got back to the room she packed everything back in her L.L. Bean tote bag as neatly as she could.

The cat rubbed against her legs.

She was sorry Bibi hadn't left a note or something.

She carried the cat downstairs with her. She liked it.

The three hounds under the kitchen table looked up with interest and thumped their tails.

"Here's your cat," she said. "What's its name? Should I feed it?"

"I've never seen that cat in my life," the foster dad said. "Get that animal out of here. Cats carry a brain-eating parasite. I don't want that cat around. Throw it out."

Stella took that cat outside and walked down the four steps from the front porch and put the cat on the ground.

"Go," she said.

The foster dad had unexpectedly followed Stella outside with a bucket full of water in one hand and a butcher knife in the other. He flung the water from the bucket in the cat's direction.

The cat yelled and ran under the porch.

"Darned thing," the foster dad said. "I'll gut it next time."

He stabbed at the air a few times with the butcher knife.

Stella had heard of people with a cat phobia and didn't judge him for it. She followed him back inside. He sat down at the kitchen table, moving his lips. He seemed to have lost interest in her. He didn't make her breakfast like he said he would. So Stella went back upstairs and collected her stuff. When she came back downstairs to say good-bye she found the foster dad in the TV room. He was watching a fuzzy program of two men folding an American flag into a neat triangle while a military band played a mournful dirge.

"Bye then," Stella said.

The foster dad looked up. He stared at Stella and frowned.

"They just played my favorite hymn, 'Nearer My God to Thee,'" he said. "They said it was the last broadcast forever. They said a cloud of deadly gas is coming our way. They've been saying the same crap on the fake news networks for days but they didn't say it on our network so we didn't believe it. We figured it was more lies. We're maybe the last ones left in the country, they say. But it's coming for us. They say it's inevitable. We're probably breathing it right now. In and out. In and out."

"Okay," Stella said.

"Mother of Prostitutes," the foster dad said. "Mother of all Abominations of the Earth. I can smell your rank carnality from here. You defile my house. You profane yourself. You shall be burnt with fire."

The foster dad's eyes glowed and his breathing grew stentorious.

"Well, bye," Stella said.

The door was on a spring and slammed behind Stella on the way out. She had just reached the end of the driveway when the cat ran out from under the porch and caught up with her. She reached down and patted it good-bye. The foster dad had come out onto the porch. He had his butcher knife. He walked down the porch steps, waving the knife slowly back and forth.

"Whoever lies with a beast shall surely be put to death," he said. "Exodus-chapter-twenty-two-verse-nineteen."

He began to walk toward Stella and the cat.

"What the heck are you talking about?" Stella said.

She was not sure why this kindly man would want to harm a cat.

The cat zipped off.

Then without any warning a bunch of dogs charged past Stella and surrounded the foster dad and bared their teeth. They growled melodiously. Their damp eyes were full of feeling. They formed a circle and closed in, walking toward the foster dad with stiffened legs. Stella didn't know what to do. "Damn you dogs, get out of here, git," the foster dad said. One of the dogs, a black chow, did not care for his tone, and it sprang forward and bit down on his arm and shook it. The foster dad cursed. He dropped his knife. He fell back and Stella heard his elbow crack. One of the other dogs bit into an ankle while the rest barked and snapped. The foster dad curled himself into a ball. He covered his face with his arms.

"Stop it, stop it!" Stella yelled.

The dogs stopped. They sat on their haunches.

"Devil-wretch," the foster dad said hoarsely. He was bleeding and crying. The dogs watched without moving as the foster dad made his way up the porch steps with his one good leg and one good elbow. He pulled himself inside and slammed the door behind. The sound of the door slamming seemed to shake the dogs from their trance and they ran up on the porch, barking and scratching at the door. Stella could hear the foster dad's three hounds barking and snarling from inside, too, and she could hear the sound of human shouts. Stella backed away. She hoped the dogs would not come after her. She hoped the foster dad was all right. She didn't have a phone to call 9-1-1. She tried to think positively but truth be told she felt rattled by the particulars of her leave-taking. Even though she was walking mostly backwards to keep an eye on the dogs she was motivated to make tracks, and soon she had put a hundred yards between herself and the wild dog pack. She could still see them on the porch, sniffing and scratching at the front door and jumping up to peek in the windows.

The cat had evidently decided that living with the foster family wasn't in its best interest, because it kept following her. Stella shooed it away but it kept coming back. She considered. She didn't want a car to hit the cat, and she knew the foster dad was not fond of it. So she scooped it up and put it in her L.L. Bean tote bag, with just its head sticking out. The cat seemed pleased about it, almost as if it had been the cat's plan all along.

Stella reached the highway. She relaxed a little. The dogs were out of sight. And a car was coming her way.

THE WOMAN IN THE CAR IS MARY MBWEMBWE, the baby said. SHE CAN'T BE TRUSTED BUT WE ARE RUNNING OUT OF TIME

The car stopped.

Stella got in.

"I am Mary Mbwembwe," the woman said. "How do you do. I like your cat. What is your name and where are you going?"

"My name is Stella," Stella said. "I'm going to Nethalem to meet my boyfriend. This isn't really my cat yet."

"Stella is a beautiful and lovely name," Mary Mbwembwe said. "I have not heard of the town of Nethalem before."

It's on the bay," Stella said.

The woman nodded.

"Then you are going my way," she said.

They drove off.

Just as Mary Mbwembwe shifted into third gear Stella saw the dogs running up on the road behind the car. The dogs were running after the car and they were barking wildly and straining to keep up.

"Strange dogs," Mary Mbwembwe said. "They sound so sad."

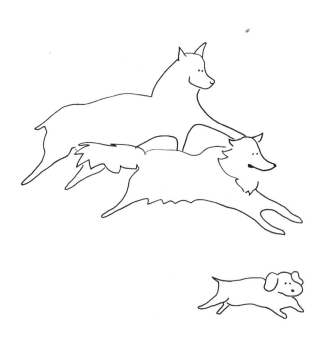

Chapter Eighteen
Margie Peach Gets to Know Her Pack

"Lordy, what a god-awful mess," Margie Peach said. "My instincts tell me I'm supposed to be with the pregnant girl who just got into that car, and I think I'm also supposed to be friends with the sad-looking woman who was driving away with her. I believe I am meant to be a part of their quest and instead I am stuck here with a pack of common dogs."

"Not me, I'm not a common dog," said a chocolate-colored lab. "I'm just trying to fit in and not make waves. I didn't want a pack of mangy stray dogs turning on me once they learned of my superior intelligence."

"What the heck?" Margie Peach said, and then she fell silent because she was flummoxed to learn that the chocolate-colored lab could speak. She had not considered the possibility, since the dog had been in the pound when they met. She concluded from the lab's superior attitude that it must be a male dog, and when she sniffed the lab's rear she was surprised to learn she had been wrong: the lab was a bitch.

"Stop that, Christ!" the lab snapped, and Margie Peach remembered herself.

"What about you other dogs? What's your pathetic story?" said the chocolate-colored lab, with bitterness and cynicism and not expecting a reply.

In rapid succession the other dogs revealed themselves to be human in origin in what soon became a cathartic circle of shared confusion and alarm, and of joy as well, because the world was more bearable now that they knew they were not alone.

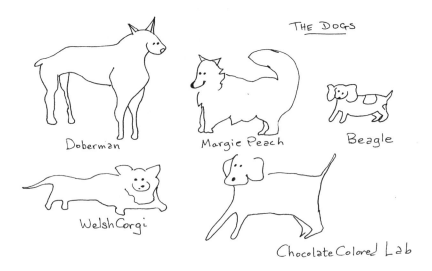

THE DOGS

Doberman

Margie Peach

Beagle

Welsh Corgi

Chocolate Colored Lab

"My name is Lois Higgenbottom, and I'm an alcoholic," the Welsh Corgi shared breathlessly. "Two days ago I was on my knees digging in my garden when the strangest feeling came over me. All over my body I felt a strong sensation of good will and joy. I ripped off my garden gloves and began to dig in the dirt with my bare hands. Then I stuck my snout into the upturned earth to catch the scent of worms and grubs. I had never smelled anything so rich and arousing before. All my senses awakened. All my aches and cares fell away."

The Welsh Corgi had upset herself by telling her own story and she began to weep. One of the other dogs tried to give her a hug, but such a human gesture coming from a dog's body seemed mawkish. Another licked the dirt from the Welsh Corgi's snout, and that seemed right to them, and so they all did it.

Next the beagle shared her story. Just that morning she had been an eleven-year-old girl with a congenital heart condition. Having a strong heart pumping in her body was still new to her, and she was so full of exuberance about the change that she ran about in circles as she spoke.

The Doberman spoke next. She told them that she was a successful televangelist and her flock numbered in the tens of thousands. As she told them her story, though, a tragic feeling grew in her, that she might possibly have been suffering from dementia in these last years, because when she tried to recall her recent sermons in detail all she could remember was a haze of never-changing routines, of meals spoon-fed to her by her son, and of visits to an adult daycare center where she passed the time shuffling cards. That morning her son had come to visit her, to bring her groceries and to check on her, and he had been met at the door by a Doberman. Naturally her son shouted and dropped the groceries on the floor; and the Doberman, ashamed, had run straight out of the open front door, never looking back.

The other dogs whined in sympathy. They licked the Doberman's face. What the Doberman did not tell them at first was that her son had appeared to her that morning as an Angel might appear, exactly as described in Ezekiel, complete with cloven hooves and four heads and six wings and a disconcertingly large and half-erect penis that was utterly on display since Angels knew no shame and rarely wore garments either on earth or in heaven. She also did not tell them that she had been filled with the hope that her Angel-son would know his own mother, even if she were a dog, and that he would take her with him to heaven in spite of her animal nature. But he rose up into the air without her, because he was one of those precious souls whom God saved first to be taken straight into Heaven in the Rapture, whereas she had been left behind, a common, soulless dog. Ever since then, the Doberman had been asking herself why her son had become the spitting image of a Cherub as described in Ezekiel and had risen up, whereas his mother, presumably in God's favor because of her lifetime of pious good works, had become a household pet. But at first she did not tell the other dogs this part of her story, because she was ashamed, and because she felt that they, like her, were damned or worse.

Margie Peach introduced herself next.

"As for me, I am a breeder of New Mexico whiptails, a species of female-only lizards that reproduces through parthenogenesis," she said. "I also study mud-dwelling freshwater meiofauna. I am an autodidact and a systematic taxonomist. I am a poet. I was born with arthrogryposis and strabismus. Now that I am a dog I realize all the more that these differences were a part of who I was. In a better world my disabilities would not have caused people to mock me as they did. In a better world I would have loved myself more. My congenital differences gave me the strength to accept my transfiguration when it came, and to love the dog I am today."

"Here, here," the Welsh Corgi said.

"If we're going to trot out our laurels I could tell you all that I'm a world-famous surgeon," said the chocolate-colored lab. "Actually it's true. I'm an Ear, Nose and Throat surgeon. People come to me from all over the world after a diagnosis of laryngeal cancer. I give them hope. Sometimes I give them a chance at life. But I'm no longer a doctor, am I? I'm a dog. I can't even hold a tongue depressor. Everyone can just call me Queenie."

"Hello, Doctor Queenie," Margie Peach said respectfully.

"No need to mock me," snapped the chocolate-colored lab. "I know I'm only a dog. Don't you get it? This is an end of the world scenario. This is an extinction-level event. Maybe because I'm a dog I feel compulsively eager to tell you the truth about our situation. It's the end of civilization, and here I am, stuck in a dog's body with you losers—with an alcoholic gardener, and an eleven-year-old kid with a heart condition, and a Holy Roller of a televangelist, and a dilettantish amateur scientist! Nothing of your past matters! That world is done! We're just dogs!"

"Hey," Margie Peach said. "I'm not just a dog. You're not just a dog. None of us are just dogs."

"We are children of God," the Doberman said. Then she looked troubled, because she was thinking about the way her son rose toward the heavens without her.

"Or else, maybe, we are the Damned," she whispered, breaking it to them as gently as she could.

"Thanks for clearing that up," the chocolate-colored lab said bitterly.

"Please, everyone, let's not turn on one another like curs," Margie Peach said. "And let's give everyone a chance to introduce themselves. We'll discuss theology later perhaps."

Just one dog hadn't spoken. The German Shepherd. Margie Peach looked at the German Shepherd expectantly and when it hesitated she nodded encouragingly. She was eager to move beyond the cynicism of the chocolate-colored lab as well as the rigid fundamentalism of the Doberman. As pack leader she knew that a bad attitude in one dog could infect the whole pack. In spite of her encouragement, though, the German Shepherd began to snarl and to back up, its tail low in a classic fear response.

"It's okay," Margie Peach said. "You don't have to share if it's not the right time, dear."

Instead of being heartened by Margie Peach's tender words, the German Shepherd barked so loudly and abruptly that a rabbit jumped out of a nearby oleander bush, and the German Shepherd snapped it up and ran away with the poor creature's entrails trailing behind.

"Oh," the Doberman said.

"I guess that one was a real dog," the Welsh Corgi said.

Chapter Nineteen
Making Friends in Time of Turmoil

Mary Mbwembwe's car was barely pasted together. The muffler dragged along on the ground. Inside the car it sounded as if they were trapped inside a tin can being banged on with a spoon. But somehow everything Mary Mbwembwe said made Stella relax a little more. The cat slept peacefully in the L.L. Bean tote bag and Stella felt her worries drift away and she was happy again.

"What is the name of your cat?"

"It doesn't have a name," Stella said.

"You're right about that," Mary Mbwembwe said. "Cats know who they are, all right."

They were traveling in that vast and vacant part of California where the only things to see out the car windows were scrubby bushes the color of lichen and dirt, plus an endless graveyard of mothballed military planes, parked for good and rusting in the desert.

They traveled west, following the setting sun.

MARY MBWEMBWE WILL BETRAY THE BEAST, the baby said.

Her baby had been quiet for some time, and the way it piped up now, flooding Stella's mind with useless information, startled her and made her sit up straight.

"What is it, what is it?" Mary Mbwembwe said. "Are you feeling some contraction or another?"

"My baby just told me something," Stella said.

"Look, girl," Mary Mbwembwe said. "You know your baby can't talk to you, right?"

Stella didn't answer. They rode on without saying anything, until they got to a narrow, curving road and turned north.

"Look, girl," Mary Mbwembwe said again, and Stella decided it must be Mary Mbwembwe's way of saying "hey," or "listen to this."

"Look, girl, there are a lot of birds up there, hey?"

"Yeah," said Stella. She didn't look though. She was feeling sleepy.

"Maybe some music is just the ticket," Mary Mbwembwe said, and she turned on the radio. A man with a robust voice came on. He was shouting through the speakers.

AMERICA USED TO BE A WHITE, CHRISTIAN, DEMOCRATIC COUNTRY. IT WAS OUR CREATION, IT WAS OUR INHERITANCE, BUT WHITE CIVILIZATION IS GONE, MY FELLOW AMERICANS. THE ANIMALS ARE WINNING.

"Do you mind if I change the station?" Stella said.

"Oh? Sure. What is this one saying? I can't really understand when they talk so fast."

"Same old stuff."

Stella pushed the 'scan' button and watched the digital numbers flash by until they came back to the same station once more.

THE PRESIDENT WARNED OF THIS, THE PRESIDENT EXPOSED IT, WE ARE ABOUT TO PLUNGE INTO ABSOLUTE, RAZOR-SHARP, TOTAL EVIL. IT'S THE END OF THE WORLD, MY FRIENDS

"He sounds very angry indeed," Mary Mbwembwe said.

"Maybe something big is happening," Stella said. "Maybe it's the end of the world. Where is all the traffic, anyway? Have you even seen a plane today?"

"Well isn't that the silliest thing I ever heard," Mary Mbwembwe said. "These radio people talk this way all the live-long day. How could it be the end of the world when there is a new baby on the way? Hmm? I'm sure there is very rarely traffic on this road. We have taken a back way."

Mary Mbwembwe turned the radio off.

A little nothing happened, a void that felt peaceful to them both.

Chapter Twenty
Major Eureka Yamanaka Catches a Glimpse of Josefina Guzman

Major Eureka Yamanaka still lugged around the nuclear football wherever she went under the Mountain. It made her nostalgic to remember all the times she had carried it when nothing much was going on in the world except the typical wars and plagues.

That morning the scientists had all tried to break out so they could get home to their families. They had made it all the way to the blast doors before they were turned back by soldiers still taking orders from the President. Now the scientists just sat back in their swivel chairs and watched as the World Map lit up in the command room. By now there were just two places on the globe that had not been ravaged by Agent-T: a thirty-mile radius around the South Pole, and an unaffected ribbon of land running straight through the vast and sprawling corporate farms of California's Central Valley. The generals concluded from the evidence that Agent-T could be defeated by pesticide. The President ordered strategic missile strikes from sea to shining sea. Each missile carried what they hoped would be a lifesaving payload of Chlorpyrifos and Metolachlor. But the only measurable outcomes of Operation Pesticide were ataxia, paralysis, and death. The plague raged on.

Two hundred soldiers still sat at their monitors in the Command Center under the mountain. The soldiers were mostly right out of basic training. They hadn't shaved for days and their eyes were bloodshot and their skin was broken out and they were bored. They sucked on their forearms while they mock-targeted National Monuments and other sites of historic interest and pretended to fire.

Major Eureka Yamanaka stood behind them, watching the feeds over their shoulders.

She saw an old woman with seagull feathers in her hair. The woman was standing on top of an abandoned shipping container at the edge of a mucky swamp and was shaking a long fishing pole at the drone, waving it off.

"Look there," Major Eureka Yamanaka said, and pointed to the screen. "That old woman with feathers in her hair. Who is that?"

"Her? Nobody," the soldier said.

"What is that place?"

"Nowhere," the soldier said. "The temperature of the water around there has gone up eighty-four degrees in the last three days, though. We've been monitoring it. That's Centigrade. The fish are boiling in the bay."

Then he steered his drone north, toward San Francisco, where traffic lights on empty streets kept up an endless progression of green, yellow, and red.

She saw flamingos flocking on the Golden Gate Bridge.

"Take out those flamingos for me, will you?" a passing colonel said.

It might have been a joke. But the soldier fired, and feathers filled the sky like a confetti parade, and the bridge sagged slowly in the middle, then collapsed.

"Well done, soldier!" the colonel said, and gave the soldier a sharp and manly slap on the back.

That did it. They had inexhaustible ordinance and they were eager to deploy some. One of the soldiers fired into a vast flock of sheep grazing in Battery Park. When the smoke cleared they saw a straggle of survivors looking stupidly over the lip of the crater. Somebody else attacked a pack of wolves roaming through Red Square and the surviving wolves turned on each other in a frenzy. Within minutes, the Taj Mahal in Agra, and the Christ the Redeemer statue in Rio, and the Colosseum in Rome, and the Astrodome in Houston were no more.

Major Eureka Yamanaka thought it pitiful to see.

When one of the soldiers asked to be relieved, she followed him. He looked sweaty and sick. Probably a dog lover, she thought. Just before he was relieved he had been ordered to blow up a poodle standing at attention on a front porch in Whitefish, Montana.

"Hi," Major Eureka Yamanaka said.

The soldier looked back over his shoulder at her. His skin was the color of a rice pancake. He had stopped shaving a while ago and his beard was straggly and adolescent. When she walked past him he followed. Her quarters had one of those prefab, single-user showers, and they both squeezed into it. It was their natural inclination to want to wash something off before coming together. When he kissed her she felt transported to a virgin planet full of wild beasts and empty of human predation. He was so confused about the nature of things that she needed to guide him all the way. His private parts were covered in downy soft peltish stuff. She accepted it. She knew what was happening to them. For days now she had been plucking quill-like growths out of her skin. The quills kept coming back and today they had tufts of feathery stuff on the ends. She had also noticed a general broadening of her shoulders. And her fingers were getting longer. She knew the air filters weren't protecting them. She resolved not to dwell on it. She resolved to adore her little furry man instead. His enthusiasm was amazing. His stamina was gerbil-like. They both knew they were doomed. It was the best sex they had ever had.

Later he laid his head on her shoulder.

"It's the end of the world, you know," he said.

Major Eureka Yamanaka considered it.

She had seen vast herds of bison reconstitute themselves and travel north across the plains. She had seen flocks of birds darkening the sky. One of the scientists had even sworn that he had spotted passenger pigeons in those massive flocks, returned from the dead. No one could explain the glimpses of living shapes that the drones picked up and fed back to them, here and there, now and then, just shadowy forms, hovering at the mysterious edges of things; shapes that the cameras always just missed, but that seemed to suggest the shapes of long-extinct species: Great Auk and Blue Buck; Dusky Flying Fox and Steller's Sea Cow; Pig-Footed Bandicoot and Great Woolly Mammoth.

Whatever was going on, Major Eureka Yamanaka decided, it wasn't a world coming to an end. Because the world was bursting with life.

"We're the Witnesses," the boy in her arms said solemnly. "We'll see it all come to pass. Next will come the Comet, called Wormwood, and after the Comet, but before the End, will come the Beast."

"What the Hell are you talking about?" Major Eureka Yamanaka said.

"My mother raised me to believe," he said. "It's all written down in the book of Revelation. Every bit, foretold."

His voice was husky and the sound of it made her feel maternal.

"My mother taught me chapter and verse. Literally. That's why I know what's coming, Major. The Orange Beast with Seven Heads and Ten Horns is coming and unless we are among the saved he will devour us."

Major Eureka Yamanaka did not argue. Instead she kissed the top of his head. And then she suggested, through gestures ranging far beyond a simple kiss, that they make the best of things for the time they had left, and without too much persuasion on her part he agreed.

The next morning she woke up alone. Her blanket looked as if it had been gnawed by a rat and the air smelled like fresh droppings. She got up and showered and dressed and went out to explore. No one was in the Command Room. She checked the President's corridor and found his door guarded by a half-dozen men who pointed their guns at her and ordered her to retreat. All of the President's men were wearing their gas masks again. It seemed a little late to Major Eureka Yamanaka to be worrying about gas masks, and she did not ask for one. Instead she wandered elsewhere, knocking on doors, and when a human voice answered they spoke together through the door, because those inside were afraid if they opened the door she might infect them.

That afternoon Major Eureka Yamanaka got a satellite receiver going, and she checked for broadcast signals on every frequency, but all she could find was a grainy broadcast of a military band playing "Nearer My God to Thee."

She kept trying to raise any signal, from anyone in the world.

She imagined there must still be places unaffected by the plague.

Nuclear submarine crews.

Science missions in Antarctica.

A beach in western Australia.

Nobody answered.

pinguinus impennis

Chapter Twenty-One
Mary Mbwembwe and Stella are Attacked by a Bird, or Maybe a Celestial Being

After a while Mary Mbwembwe began to sing as she drove along, at first slow and low and shy, and then rising, until she was singing in a way that sounded to Stella like a lullaby.

"That's pretty," Stella said.

"All of Africa loves this song," Mary Mbwembwe said. "It was written by the famous Prince Niko Mbarga, and it was made even more famous by the famous Miriam Makeba. It is called 'Sweet Mother.' And that is exactly the kind of mother you are going to be."

Stella began to feel optimistic.

"Look girl, you sing, too," said Mary Mbwembwe, and when Stella said that she didn't sing except when no one else was around, Mary Mbwembwe insisted, and then she taught the song to Stella, one note following the next, until the two of them sounded like drunken sailors.

"You see," said Mary Mbwembwe. "You do sing."

Mary Mbwembwe sighed. The world felt right to them both and the inside of the car was glowing in the final sunset moments of the day.

"So it seems to me that you are maybe running away from home," Mary Mbwembwe said. "How are you getting along on the road?"

"All right," Stella said. "I can take care of myself."

"Yes," said Mary Mbwembwe. "I can see you are a very strong girl, and I can see you will be a very good mother."

Stella decided to believe it.

Inside the car was blank and warm. Stella rolled her window down. They had been very lucky on the route because there wasn't a bit of traffic anywhere. They could pretend the whole world was theirs, and that this road was their very own personal road. Stella stuck her hand out. Warm air rushed over her skin and pushed against her hand and everything felt blessedly normal. They passed many industrial farms, and a private prison complex or two, and all of them were silent and still. Then they began to climb into the hills. The hilltops were covered with monstrous windmills, one row after another. All motionless. There was no wind at all. None except what the car made, speeding through the still air.

"Ah, then," Mary Mbwembwe said. "And when is the baby due?"

"Pretty soon."

"And this boy of yours, does he know you're on your way? Is there somebody on the other side to catch you, girl?"

Stella didn't say anything.

"I get it," said Mary Mbwembwe. "What does your mother say? Was she unkind to you?"

"My mother doesn't know," she said. "My mother is in jail."

"Ah."

"To tell you the truth my mother loves me a lot," Stella said. "She just had bad luck all around."

"I know about bad luck, exactly," Mary Mbwembwe said.

Soon they were driving through a darkening valley that was full of industrial buzzing although there was no industry. The sky was red and the sun and the moon had sunk into the night and they left the whole world glowing in a primordial-looking twilight.

On a whim Stella opened her pink book, thinking, in a superstitious way to be sure, that it might give her guidance about how Lix Tetrax would feel to see her show up at his door. Her little pink pocket Bible fell open and she read: THE BEAST STOOD BEFORE THE WOMAN WHICH WAS READY TO BE DELIVERED, FOR TO DEVOUR HER CHILD AS SOON AS IT WAS BORN.

"Well, that can't be good," she murmured. "Honestly I had no idea that religious people had such violent beliefs."

She put the book away, in her L.L. Bean tote bag, under the cat.

The birds were back. They covered the sky.

"That's very strange," Mary Mbwembwe said, but she did not explain.

The flock seemed to grow by the second, and it seemed to include all kinds of birds—seagull, turkey vulture, sparrow, cardinal, crow—

WATCH OUT, the baby said.

A ghostly silver limo was hurtling toward them on the wrong side of the road and the driver was like no one Stella had ever seen: white-haired and red-eyed and with brilliant wings sprouting from the shoulders—wings so large that they stuck out the open windows on both sides.

Mary Mbwembwe screamed and turned the wheel.

The car spun out, and then rolled over and over as if slapped by a giant hand.

Stella was upside-down, hanging by the shoulder strap.

URNBAY INWAY ELLHAY UCKINGFAY ANGELWAY OUYAY ANTKAY TOPSAY EEMAY, the baby said.

Hearing her baby's voice, Stella felt relief so strong she laughed. Her laugh sounded strangely liquid.

"Mary Mbwembwe?" she said.

Nobody answered. She couldn't turn her head to see.

Someone tried to open her crushed door.

"Are you all right?" a voice said, upside down, through the shattered window.

"I'm pregnant. I was traveling with a very nice lady and a cat," Stella said. "Please help them first. I'm okay. My baby is okay."

She heard a prying metal sound.

"Careful, she's pregnant!" said a voice.

"I keep calling 9-1-1 and no one answers!"

"Did anyone get the license number?"

Someone cut her seat belt strap and many arms caught her. Stella looked up into the kindly faces of the people leaning over her. They laid her gently on the ground next to Mary Mbwembwe and looked her over. Mary Mbwembwe's eyes were closed. There was a VW Bus parked in the road. On its side was painted "Fresno Trans Glee Choir" in violet letters.

"Stay calm!" somebody said. "Everything is going to be all right! We're going to get an ambulance out here! Why don't they answer?"

ODIUM ENIM EST OPTIMA ANIMI, the baby said.

"Let me through! I know CPR!" somebody shouted .

"Help Mary Mbwembwe!" Stella said.

"We need you to stay calm," a voice said. "Please, Miss, please."

An ambulance came. It was the last time ever in this world that an ambulance would come, but the people did not know it yet, and they did not commemorate the moment.

Book Five

To the Abyss

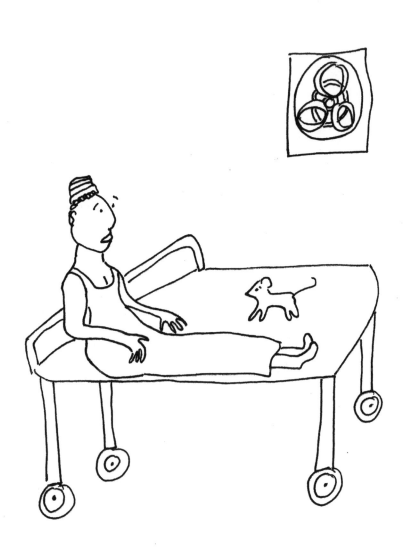

Chapter Twenty-Two
Mary Mbwembwe Draws on the Lessons of Her Past

Even Mary Mbwembwe had trouble understanding the next things that happened after she found herself rolling over and over in her car, and then gliding weightlessly toward a bright white light at the end of a tunnel, and then being subjected to a vigorous pumping on her chest that may have cracked a rib or two, and then finding herself turning back from the light to return to this earth. Through closed lids and while traversing the land between the dead and the living she saw a vision of a pregnant girl wearing a dress with suns on it and a twelve-starred crown on her head. She saw a seven-headed, ten-horned, orange-colored Beast rising up from a hole in the ground. She saw dogs reciting poetry, and bears reading books. She saw herself, too, but as a swift black panther, and she felt her mind become cat-like. And then she was awake, fully awake, and in an ambulance, with the pregnant girl on the gurney next to hers.

"Don't worry, keep breathing," a woman with a mask over her face said to her, and Mary Mbwembwe took this advice to heart as a valuable life lesson.

When they got to the hospital she and Stella were rolled in opposite directions and Mary Mbwembwe lost sight of her young pregnant friend. Two burly women in smocks rolled her down a wide bright hallway at maximum speed. They were running in a way that made Mary Mbwembwe feel as if her life would soon be over in spite of their best efforts. She could feel the torque every time they turned a corner and she thought she might tumble out each time.

125

Then she stopped with a jerk.

Somebody stuck a drip in her arm.

They went away.

Nobody came, not for a long time.

Then longer still.

Mary Mbwembwe waited patiently. The drip drained.

She heard gunshots from the lower floors. Booted feet were coming up the stairwell in her direction. Mary Mbwembwe ripped out the IV. She thought quickly—where to run? Or alternatively, where to hide?—and then she did the best thing given current circumstances and covered her head with the sheet. She played dead. She heard screams, grunts, giggles, and unidentifiable screeches. More gunfire. What sounded like thunder, followed by many feet running by, only inches away. She opened her eyes and through the sheet she saw galloping four-legged shapes running past on all fours. The smell of rut and blood filled the air.

Then all was still.

Mary Mbwembwe, too, was still, for a long time.

Nothing happened for at least seven hours.

She moved the sheet with imperceptible, patient slowness from her face.

Then she sat up and looked around.

Chapter Twenty-Three
Wanda Lubiejewski Witnesses the Apocalypse from a Bear's Perspective

Now that Wanda Lubiejewski and her daughter were big glorious muscular creatures covered with opulent fur they felt an overwhelming urge to run north, following a scent on the air that called to them and compelled them forward.

"Why?" her daughter asked.

Wanda Lubiejewski asked herself the question. Why run north? Was it instinct? Was it some ancestral, bearish memory driving them in that direction? Were they polar bears?

And as she asked herself these questions, into her mind came the shadowy shapes of a pregnant girl, and a goat, and a giant bird, and a Beast with seven heads.

Wanda Lubiejewski wasn't sure if what she saw in her head was just an overactive imagination or if it genuinely meant something.

"Something is waiting for us," she told her child. "I don't know what."

"Okay," her daughter said, and trusted her mother.

Wanda Lubiejewski warned her child to stay hidden from all humans. Otherwise the humans might decide to shoot the girl, out of fear or for sport. Wanda Lubiejewski was a mother in a world that was becoming ever more unpredictable and savage, and her child was a bear with teeth the size of jackhammers and who stood twelve feet high at the shoulder. Wanda thought people might have unnecessary prejudice toward her child. She thought that they might react with fear and hate, the way humans often do when confronted with a creature that they can't control or dominate. She and her child traveled only at night. They avoided roads and cleared places and followed the riparian curves of the landscape instead, where trees and bush gave them cover.

Their need to stay hidden slowed their progress. They were still far to the south and east from their destination when the Great Battle of the Central Valley began with a clash of cymbals and a crash of horns. The shrieks and cries of the battlefield drove them even further off-course. They traveled from stream to river to wood, making very little real progress because their way was so roundabout.

Then one night the two bears were startled by a lone helicopter passing low over their heads, almost scraping the trees and with its searchlight blaring.

In the next moment a dozen helicopters filled the sky with so much brightness and noise and smell that Wanda and her daughter could no longer see or hear or smell. They were running blind.

In their confusion they ran straight out of the concealment of the trees and onto a road full of commotion and weeping. There were trucks crammed full of people. There were animals of all kinds being rounded up into separate trucks. There were men shouting through megaphones. There were men with guns. And it was the moment of darkest crisis for a mother because she knew her child was going to be shot and killed at any moment and that there was nothing she could do.

But no one paid a bit of attention to them. No one shot, or even threatened to shoot. The trauma of these people's lives was already so great, and the reality of their circumstances so impossible, that they had no will to react even when two monstrous bears plunged into their midst. They were already overwhelmed by the facts.

Only after Wanda and her daughter had run back to the safety of the trees did one of the men think to fire his gun, a single shot, and he shot a window out of one of the trucks, and no one was hurt.

No one came after them.

They were safe.

But Wanda could no longer find the scent they had been following.

They were lost.

Chapter Twenty-Four
Fight Every Which Way You Can

During her first hours in the hospital Stella got rolled over in bed like a pig on a spit while various catheters got emptied and replaced in a purgatory of procedure performed by people who never talked or looked at her.

She fell asleep.

Stella dreamed of her mother.

Uncharacteristically her mother had assumed the shape of a Great Woolly Mammoth, and her mother's earthy scent filled the dream so fully that, whenever Stella breathed in, she felt like an animal herself, with thick fur and scary jaws and legs like tree trunks. Since Stella was dreaming, why not, she decided to imagine enormous wings for herself. The two beasts looked at one another. The look was confrontational but loving. It had always been that way between these two.

"I don't get why you're coming to see me in a dream, Mom," Stella said.

"It's my only choice, bunny," the Great Woolly Mammoth said. "I'm here to deliver a message. You'll forget the dream but I will still be there with you, inside, and my message will give you serenity and strength for the trials to come."

"Whatever," Stella said. She knew it was just a dream. And she was used to her mother not following through on her best intentions.

The Great Woolly Mammoth looked her up and down, the way mothers do, especially when looking at pregnant teen daughters.

"Listen to me, Stella," her mother said. "You've suffered a traumatic brain injury. That's what the doctors said before they all ran away. Spelled T, B, I. Your brain got shook. You're going to hear the voices even louder than before. You'll think you're having conversations with people who aren't there. You'll have delusions of grandeur. You'll feel like you're facing laughably impossible challenges and you'll think that you and your friends are the only ones who can save the world and you'll be right."

"What do I do, Mom?"

The Great Woolly Mammoth rested her furry trunk on Stella's forehead, as if checking her temperature.

"All of you need to work together or you don't stand a chance," the Great Woolly Mammoth said. "It will take all six of you. Working together."

"All of who?" Stella said.

"All of you losers," the Great Woolly Mammoth said. "The undocumented and disabled. The forgotten ones. The left behinds. The last will be first. It's our turn. All of you need to fight together, every which way you can, and then some, and then some more, and even after you do all that, you will probably fail, and then die."

"Your advice feels problematic and unworkable," Stella said. "What the heck are you talking about, Mom?"

The Great Woolly Mammoth didn't answer, but Stella felt the creature's soft breath, warming her from her soul to her toes, and she slept more deeply, and then she woke up.

She became aware of this new idea: that no one had rolled her over for some hours, or days, maybe.

She became aware of not hearing bright steps on the hard shiny floors in the hallways, or hearing call buttons make the alarms ring for the nurses to come, or smelling either bedpans or flower baskets being carried down the hall.

All of these impressions had stopped.

She was alone.

She decided to sleep some more.

Then nobody still came. Not for a long time.

Her baby said: WAKE UP, WAKE UP, WAKE UP!

She woke up. She didn't know what year it was.

She slept.

She was aware of time passing. She was drifting in a hazy sea of despair. As it was with many young people in those times, her life had become floaty and directionless.

In the twilight haze of some other time, while dozing in a hopeless and despairing sort of way, she felt a presence standing next to her bed.

OPEN YOUR EYES, her baby said.

Stella thought: "My mom is here."

She opened her eyes.

"Oh, it's you," Stella said. "We had an accident."

"Everyone is gone," Mary Mbwembwe said. "I learned from the radio that there has been a therianthropic chemical attack. Everyone has fled the scene. There have been gun battles between Angels and Beasts in the very halls of this hospital. In the chaos and the subsequent Rapture you and I have been left behind. That is what I heard, before the broadcasts ceased. That we have experienced a therianthropic chemical attack, followed by a Rapture."

"Thank you for telling me but everything you say sounds impossible," Stella said.

"Oh no," Mary Mbwembwe said. "There is looting in the streets. Cities are on fire. Wild animals have invaded our cities. Angel sightings are through the roof. Military men came through and rounded up the people and put them in trucks and drove them away. They must have left you as a goner. As for myself, I hid under a sheet. You are not in labor I hope."

"Oh please let's not talk about this conspiracy stuff any longer," Stella said. "My aunt's boyfriend says the chemtrails are brainwashing us into believing all kinds of crazy stuff. Or maybe it's secret signals coming through the electric grid or the cell phone towers. I've heard it all. I'm hurt. I have traumatic brain injury. I have no clothes except this hospital gown with these tiny smiley-faced suns on it and it leaves me bare-assed in back. I feel sick. I feel terrible. I'm going to call the nurse now with this handy call-button."

"I think we should skedaddle," Mary Mbwembwe said. "Since you are feeling burdened by your cares, I will locate a wheelchair."

Mary Mbwembwe left the room and came back with a wheelchair. She slid her left arm under both of Stella's legs and her right arm behind Stella's back and then without knowing how it happened Stella found herself sitting in the wheelchair.

"You can see how I excel at this kind of work," Mary Mbwembwe said. "I am trained as a Certified Nurse's Aide. I take care of old wealthy people as my profession. I will tell you a story one day, maybe."

And with that she took a wide-toothed hair pick out of her pocket and she fussed with Stella's hair and then she patted Stella's cheek and then she looked at her so lovingly that Stella felt sure everything would be all right, after all.

"Ok, but where is my stuff?" Stella said. "I had a bag. I had shoes. I had a handy pair of kitchen shears. I had meds. I had a cat. I had cash. I had a package of Hostess Donettes."

Mary Mbwembwe handed Stella her L.L. Bean tote bag.

"It was hanging in the cupboard here by your bed," she said.

The bag was empty except for her aunt's kitchen shears and her little pink Bible.

"Where are my clothes? Where are my meds?" she said. "Where is my cat? Where is my cash? Where are my Hostess Donettes?"

"I guess your clothes were covered with blood from our accident and probably not so good any longer. Your meds and Hostess Donettes and money are probably stolen. We must hope for the best for your cat. Now here is our plan. I will roll you very gently down the corridor. Please tell me if you experience any discomfort."

Mary Mbwembwe began to roll Stella in a very steady way and not at all like they were in danger. The journey to the elevator was unremarkable. There was no one in the hallway. The television was on in the waiting room and the test pattern flickered. The elevator came and it was empty except for the messages of death and doom scrawled across its walls.

"Do you really think we should be taking the elevator in times such as these?" Stella said.

Mary Mbwembwe didn't answer. She pushed the button for the lobby and the doors closed and they began to go down. Stella's heart jumped when the doors opened on the second floor, but it was only a harassed-looking woman wearing a red polo shirt and spotless white slacks, and she got into the elevator and said to Mary Mbwembwe: "Are you the doctor on call? My sister is injured. We've been waiting in the emergency room for hours. No one is helping us. A squirrel bit her. There is no one to help."

Mary Mbwembwe patted the other woman's shoulder reassuringly.

"Go be with your sister," she said. "Everything will be all right."

"I'm almost ready to give up and take her across town to the urgent care clinic but the wait there might be even longer," the woman said. "It's in that part of town. Always crowded with the uninsured."

"Don't worry," Mary Mbwembwe said. "All will be well."

The woman thanked her tersely. She was still full of dissatisfaction. But Mary Mbwembwe felt she could do no more for her, under the circumstances. The elevator doors opened. The hospital lobby was empty except for trash and overturned chairs. The woman walked to the left to find her sister, and Mary Mbwembwe pushed Stella to the right, toward the exit. The door to the outside world was stuck open and the glass was broken. Mary Mbwembwe guided the wheelchair through the open door. It was dark outside and the halogen lights in the parking lot blinked and sputtered and made the world look exactly like a black-and-white zombie movie.

"I thought it would be daytime for some reason," Stella said.

"It's been dark for three days," Mary Mbwembwe said. "Or maybe not. Maybe it's just what I think. What is a day, really, in such circumstances? My watch has stopped working."

Stella's eyes adjusted. The sky was pulsing. Some deer were in the parking lot, pulling the leaves off of the potted trees with their lips. The deer swung their heads up and sniffed the air with their moist black noses. Then they trotted right over and began to follow behind the wheelchair. Stella decided to be all right with it. It was creepy but at least they were herbivores.

"Where is your car?" Stella said.

"Silly girl. My car is no longer any good. There was an accident."

Stella lost hope. But Mary Mbwembwe just kept rolling Stella along in her same long slow steady way, a method perfected after many years of caring for old people. She kept on going until they came to a bus stop three blocks away.

"Look, Mary, I don't know if we can count on this bus schedule," Stella said.

"Time will tell," Mary Mbwembwe said.

The bus didn't come, but a cat did, and it looked so much like the cat that had followed Stella from Bibi's house that Stella said, "Hey! I think that's my cat!"

"Son of a gun," Mary Mbwembwe said.

Stella opened her L.L. Bean tote bag wide and the cat trotted over and jumped right in and settled itself comfortably. It looked relieved to be back where it belonged.

"This cat is a small miracle," Mary Mbwembwe said. "I will take it as a sign of our coming good fortune."

Something blew up in the next block.

A pack of dogs trotted toward them, with heads lowered meekly and with tails wagging, a black chow leading.

That was when a flatbed truck drove up to the bus stop and an old woman leaned out.

"I'm charging five dollars a mile." she said. She had a sixteen-gauge shotgun draped casually across her lap.

"Per passenger, that is," she said.

"Good woman," Mary Mbwembwe said solemnly. "Surely you can see we are barreling toward the End Times. If ever there is a time to be a Good Samaritan, this would be it. Helping this poor pregnant girl could be your last chance to tip the scales before you are judged."

Stella was impressed at how mellifluous her friend's language could become in a pinch. The woman with the sixteen-gauge shotgun looked humble and contrite.

"All righty," the woman said. "Climb aboard and buckle up."

The truck was crowded with other refugees and there was no room for the wheelchair so they left it. Stella and Mary squeezed in with the others. Stella began to shiver. Something was on her mind. She kept thinking that her mother might have been left behind in jail, when the panic hit.

"No, girl, that would never happen," Mary Mbwembwe said, when Stella told her. "Any mother of yours would find a way. She would find a way because she would be thinking of her precious daughter, and how her precious daughter needs a mother's help. I know the way of mothers."

"I can't see it that way at all," Stella said. "When I think of her, it's like I see a rabbit trapped in a hutch. I see a dog without water in a kennel. I see my mother behind bars, without water or food, waiting for someone with keys who never comes."

Mary Mbwembwe shook her head vigorously.

"I tell you what," Mary Mbwembwe said. "If your mother, Stella's mother, the mother of the girl I know here, needed to get free from her jail cell, there is no way would she become a trapped rabbit. She would find her way out. She would become something very small and wise and cunning and slip out through the bars. A hummingbird. Or something highly flexible. A boa constrictor. I hear boa constrictors are very clever about squeezing themselves through tough spaces."

"Or something very large," Stella said. "I wonder. A giant elephant. A Great Woolly Mammoth. If she turned into a Great Woolly Mammoth then my mother could break down the walls and set everyone else free too."

"Yes, that is exactly what happened," Mary Mbwembwe said.

Chapter Twenty-Five
The Chocolate-Colored Lab Makes a Surprising First Impression

Because it is often difficult for dogs to track people in an Apocalypse, Margie Peach and her pack wandered and roamed and sniffed and backtracked and sometimes gave up all hope of finding Stella, all through that longest night when the sun forgot to come up, and then they pressed on, the way dogs do, until their noses finally brought them to a hospital parking lot, where at last they caught up with Stella's overpowering and glorious scent, even though she was seven floors up and the dogs were still a hundred yards away from the entrance.

They rejoiced at their good fortune. Some of the dogs wanted to rush in rashly, so that they could reunite with Stella right away. They were convinced that Providence must have brought them there, rather than their special tracking abilities, and that Providence would surely keep looking after them even if they ran straight through a crowded hospital to find her. But their pack leader Margie Peach told them to wait, and so they hid themselves in some box-berry bushes. They waited as men with guns stormed the hospital. They waited as they heard gunfire inside the hospital, followed by the lamentations of the injured or the damned. They waited as men began to rise up in the Rapture, dropping their energy drinks and Big Gulps to splash right there in the hospital parking lot where the drinks would leave big splotches of red and brown and blue for all eternity. Their patience was rewarded. At long last they smelled Stella coming closer, and then they saw her come out.

A tall stately woman wearing a white turban was pushing Stella in a wheelchair.

Margie Peach signaled to the other dogs that it was time.

They approached meekly, tails wagging.

But just before Margie Peach could introduce herself properly, Stella and the woman climbed into the back of a truck and drove away.

"Damn it," Margie Peach said, and then she apologized to her pack for her language.

"Sorry, bitches," she said. "I didn't want to scare Stella, like we did last time, so I took my time, and now look, she is getting away from us again."

The dogs followed the truck doggedly. They cheered up when they discovered that the road was so crowded with abandoned cars, dead bodies, and other stuff that they had no trouble keeping up.

A few deer fell in with Margie Peach and her pack, almost as if the deer thought they were dogs. Margie tried to communicate with them but their answers did not make any sense to her. They might have been actual deer. Or they might have been people too overcome by recent events to speak with any sort of coherence. Or it could be that their deer throats and teeth and lips had morphological differences that prevented them from forming comprehensible words. Margie Peach considered every possibility. Whatever the truth was, she felt very kindly toward these gentle animals. It startled her to realize how warmly she felt toward creatures that only a few hours ago she might have classified as meat. She tried to say hello. But while the dogs' speech was easy to understand—if moist and sloppy—the deer could only manage breathy squeaks, so Margie Peach gave up.

She next trained her attention on Stella, in the truck, and also on the woman wearing the white turban. She did not want to lose sight of either one of them ever again. There were many bad-smelling people in the back of the truck, and it was difficult to keep focused on those two, surrounded as they were by the scent of sweat and resignation.

Margie Peach knew that she and her pack might be called upon at any moment to save Stella and the turban-wearing woman from an unknown threat, and her ears pricked and the hair on the ridge of her back bristled.

A comet streaked its way all across the sky.

The truck lurched to a halt and threw all the people together, screaming.

The truck did not move again.

"What the Hell?" a man finally said, and climbed out of the truck and pulled open the driver's-side door.

A crow flew out and up into the night, squawking.

Apart from the crow, now flown, the cab was empty.

Margie Peach was not surprised. She had expected the woman driving the truck would turn out to be a crow. The only surprise was that it had taken so long. Margie Peach was developing a theory that some humans were more susceptible to Agent-T than others, just as some humans were more susceptible to rare tropical diseases.

"The driver has run off," the man said. "But she left her shotgun."

In an alarming turn of events he grabbed the gun from the seat and cocked it and pointed it at the people in the back of the truck. Margie cursed silently. She was still underestimating the way danger could flare out from any direction in this new and unfamiliar world.

"Get out," said the man, and he waved the shotgun at the people in the back of the truck. The people scrambled out and then they stood there like plastic mannikins because they were afraid to run away in case he meant to shoot them in the back. It was apparent to Margie Peach that the man had never held a gun in his life. Also, he was wearing glasses. Also, his glasses were broken. One of the lenses was cracked through. She concluded that he was unlikely to hit any target on purpose. She considered charging him. She quickly weighed the options.

141

"The gun went off and the woman in the white turban fell to the ground."

"Somebody's going to get hurt," whispered the chocolate-colored lab, because she had experience with firearms and knew the signs.

The lab was right: the gun went off and the woman wearing the white turban fell to the ground. Stella screamed and fell to her knees. The other people and the deer ran away. In the next alarming turn of events, the man with broken glasses raised the gun toward the dogs and squinted through the gun's sight, aiming. Margie Peach signaled to her pack to "sit" and they all sat. Margie Peach prayed that the man would take their thumping tails as a sign of goodwill. Perplexed and slightly crazed, the man stared at the dogs, and then stared at the injured woman, as a bloom of blood slowly spread across her chest. Then the man whispered, "I'm sorry, I'm sorry, I'm sorry," and climbed into the truck and slammed the door and drove away.

"I can help," the chocolate-colored lab said, and she ran forward to where Mary Mbwembwe lay. The lab was an ear nose and throat specialist and so it could not be said that shotgun wounds were a direct area of expertise. But she knew enough to sniff the wound and to check for signs of pneumothorax. Mary Mbwembwe's eyes widened as the dog came near and she cried out in soft ululations. Stella tried to push the lab away. The dog did not take offense.

"As long as we avoid a collapsed lung, the wound will not be fatal," the chocolate-colored lab said. "Keep pressure on the wound, Stella, until I come back. Both hands."

Stella did as she was told.

She asked: "Are you talking? Did you say my name?"

But the dogs had all run away.

sceloglaux albifacies

Chapter Twenty-Six
Stella Meets and Old Friend in Unexpected Circumstances

Stella kept both hands pressing on those parts of Mary Mbwembwe where the blood spurted most energetically. She had never felt so alone. It crossed her mind now and then that she was following the instructions of a dog but she couldn't dwell on it. Mary Mbwembwe's face had turned the color of chalk mixed with sweat and she was squeezing her eyes shut and sucking air through her teeth. Her body shimmered. She looked exactly as if she were preparing for the longest journey. The two of them were all alone and they were without hope in a world lurching on a determined course toward the end. Stella's baby wasn't helping at all. But neither was the baby making sarcastic remarks, so that was one thing she could feel grateful for. Stella wanted to say the right words to comfort Mary Mbwembwe, but the only things that came to mind were either overly literal—*gosh you have a lot of blood coming out of you*—or embarrassing clichés—*don't you die on me now.* Thankfully the dogs came back quickly. All of the dogs except for the chocolate-colored lab were carrying a giant American flag in their mouth, the size you used to see flying in front of Ford dealerships. The lab on the other hand had come back with a proper emergency medical kit, which impressed Stella very much.

"Luckily I was able to locate an Asherman Chest Seal Dressing back at the hospital," the dog said. It was not what Stella was expecting to hear from the mouth of a dog, no matter how strange the circumstances in which she found herself. The dog applied the bandage with its front paws and then sealed the bandage with delicate movements of tooth and tongue. Mary Mbwembwe looked on acceptingly, calmed by the notion that she was probably already dead. Then the dog gave Mary Mbwembwe antibiotics and a healthy dose of morphine sulphate. When the doctor was done, the other dogs spread the flag reverently on the ground. They eased Mary Mbwembwe onto the flag and then they picked up the corners in their teeth and began to carry her off, the way med techs might carry a wounded soldier from the field of battle. The cat leaped in and settled between Mary Mbwembwe's ankles, happy for the ride. Although Stella was still woozy from her recent coma, and befuddled by the behavior of these dogs, which were—let's face it—not behaving in an ordinary manner—she felt strong, almost as if it were all meant to happen, and she followed the dogs, grateful to have found such intrepid friends in her time of need.

As for Mary Mbwembwe, she felt light, almost weightless. Her trauma combined with the morphine sulfate had lifted the weight of her cares from her soul. The dogs had finally settled into a rhythm and her ride became surprisingly comfortable, unlike in the beginning, when they had jostled her plenty. Her outlook began to improve. Lying on her back, while being carried along by these dogs, she saw the night sky in a wholly new way. There were so many stars and so many birds that it looked as if the stars and birds flowed together in one continues celebration of light and flying creatures.

"Beautiful," she said.

The best place to take an injured woman would be right back to the hospital, the chocolate-colored lab argued. But her pack leader refused to backtrack under any circumstances. Margie Peach led the group onward. Not so much time passed before they came to a Marriott Hotel. Its big red sign still beamed out from the roof as if nothing at all had happened lately to affect the tourism industry. All the lobby windows were broken and the first floor was overrun with *rodentia*, but the electricity was working. Margie Peach led them up

146

to the penthouse suite, where they set Mary Mbwembwe carefully down on the bed.

At once Mary Mbwembwe fell into a deep and healing sleep. All of them felt relief. They had done the best they could under trying circumstances, and they all felt instinctively that now was a time of rest. The Welsh Corgi checked out the minibar and discovered she could open the tiny bottles with her teeth. The other dogs wandered the halls and stairways, looking for allies, and when they found none they came back and bathed one another in the monstrously large tub and then they took turns drying themselves with the hair dryer.

Stella felt as if she were trapped in the throws of a fever dream but she decided it was the best possible way to feel when in the company of possessed dogs, and she resolved not to lose heart. She sat by the bed, holding Mary Mbwembwe's hand. One of the dogs, the black chow, stood guard on the other side of the bed, every once in a while extending a paw to check Mary Mbwembwe's forehead for fever.

The dog nodded to Stella.

Then it spoke.

"My name is Margie Peach and I breed whip-tail lizards," the dog said, and the girl, too overwhelmed to react with fear or surprise, embraced the dog warmly, and sunk her face into the dog's soft fur, and felt as if she had found a long-lost friend.

Chapter Twenty-Seven
People Carrying Flashlights

On the night of the Comet, Josefina Guzman dreamed a very important dream about two giant bears and a Great Woolly Mammoth. Although these animals couldn't talk, they sang to her, and Josefina Guzman knew it was a warning.

She woke up knowing that something powerful was gathering in the dark all around her. She opened her eyes and looked.

The bears and the Great Woolly Mammoth were nowhere to be seen, but a musky smell lingered, and the odor was familiar, and it comforted her.

She heard a sound and got up from her bed. Josefina Guzman had gone to bed fully dressed as was her custom and so she felt ready to face what was coming. Her boots were still on. She walked out to meet her fate.

She saw weak beams of light, far down the dirt path in the direction of town, but coming closer. People carrying flashlights were coming toward her along the path. They weren't running in panic. They were walking quickly, though, and stiffly, as if evacuating a place that was going to be overcome by disaster any minute. Leading the group was Father Juan del Rosario. He was carrying a golden dish with a cover on it. A woman walking behind him was carrying a tall golden cross. A man walking next to the woman carrying the tall golden cross was carrying a giant Bible with a golden cover, the one that Father Juan Del Rosario always used when reading the Gospel.

"Soldiers came through the village in tanks," Father Juan del Rosario said. "They were wearing gas masks. They were rounding us up. They rounded up our animals and shot them. They set fire to the houses."

His face was black and his eyebrows singed and he looked like the devil. His clerical collar had sprung from its place and hung from his neck.

"We hid in the sacristy, and then we came here. I don't think they followed. The path is overgrown. You are not on any map."

"Who were they? Soldiers? Deportation force?" Josefina Guzman said.

Father Juan del Rosario shook his head.

"I don't know," he said. "I kept trying to call the Bishop. I tried many other numbers and no one answered anywhere, not the police, not the fire department, not my sister's home in Buenos Aires. "

Josefina Guzman counted maybe seventy people with the priest. Children were carrying other children. Old people had collapsed on the ground and sat with hunched shoulders, weeping. Josefina Guzman was at a loss. She looked down the path to see if any bad people had followed. The path was not much more than a deer trail, so lightly traveled that it was overhung with blackberry vines and thorns in places. Poison oak and scotch broom seemed to spring up overnight, and the growing things on the path seemed unusually thick and strong that year. Maybe things grew better here because they were living on one of those Superfund sites. Josefina Guzman watched the vines twist and grow and join together in the dark until there was barely a hint of a path left at all.

"I don't think they saw us leave. I think they went the other way, toward the city," Father Juan del Rosario said. He looked all done in.

"Come on," Josefina Guzman said. "Let's get you people settled."

She didn't have much to share. The fish had all died mysteriously three days before, when the water in the bay had begun to boil, and ever since she had been living on mushrooms and miner's lettuce.

"Where the heck will I find food for all these people?" she asked herself.

Overhearing her, a young boy handed her five corn tortillas wrapped in wax-paper and two cans of *huitlacoche.* The rest of them had apparently come away empty-handed. She thanked the boy, and took the five corn tortillas and the two cans of *huitlacoche,* and started to share it with the rest of the people. The food seemed to muliply mysteriously until they were all feeling sated. After they had eaten, Father Juan del Rosario took the golden dish and the golden cross and the giant Bible with the golden cover and placed them all with reverence on Josefina Guzman's white stone. The stone was an enormous block of granite, and always had been, and Josefina Guzman scolded herself for ever imagining that it was a small stone

that she could carry in her pocket. It looked like an altar, as a matter of fact. It seemed the perfect thing. Everyone genuflected. Father Juan del Rosario began to say the Mass. The familiar ritual made them all feel better right away because it allowed them to pour godly thoughts into their heads rather than to dwell on recent unpleasant events.

But just when Father Juan del Rosario came to the Kyrie Eleison, a streaking flash of light drew a jagged zipper of fire across the sky, the biggest falling star with the biggest tail on it that Josefina Guzman had ever seen, and Father Juan del Rosario seemed to forget the words.

"Wormwood," Father Juan del Rosario said hoarsely.

"Wow, that is quite a comet," the young man named Francisco said. Unlike the others he had not dropped to his knees and he was not praying incoherently with the rest of them, either, because he was still young enough to believe in the power of rational and manly thinking. "Maybe it's a falling satellite," he said. "Maybe it's aliens. It looks on a path to fall into the ocean. Maybe a tsunami is coming."

"What is Wormwood, Father?" Josefina Guzman said.

"It's the comet that comes just before the world ends," Father Juan del Rosario said. And he quoth: *The third angel blew his trumpet, and a great star fell from the sky, burning like a torch. It fell on one-third of the rivers and on the springs of water. And the name of the star is called Wormwood.*

"Please don't worry yourself about such things, Father," Josefina Guzman said. "Nobody believes that part of the Bible, not even our Father in Rome. I'm sure the streak across the sky was just a satellite. Probably it's just a satellite."

She patted his arm. The priest looked very young to her and she was sorry to see him in the thrall of the more superstitious elements of their religion. Eventually he began to say the Mass from where he had left off. Tears streamed down his plump brown clean-shaven cheeks. His return to the familiar rite seemed to give them all solace, even if Father Juan del Rosario stumbled over the words now and then, and cried out in despair without warning, and beat his breast with horrible conviction during the Agnus Dei.

Josefina Guzman felt responsible for them all, even the priest, who was after all still a young man, far from his home in Argentina. At least it seemed that no one had followed the priest and his people from the town. Maybe they were all under God's protection. Maybe it was going to be all right after all. In the morning things would look up, no doubt. Josefina Guzman hoped for the best. Little by little they settled in. They were too exhausted and terrorized to do much more than fall asleep wherever they could find a dry spot to lie down. Josefina Guzman fell asleep too, and her dreams were filled with animals: foxes, badgers, herons, two bears, and countless dogs; and the animals gathered around her as she slept and they wished her strength and victory in the battle to come, and when Josefina Guzman asked them, "What battle do you mean, and why are you bothering a forgotten old woman with your nonsense?" they nodded sagely and ran away into the reeds.

The next morning all the people were gone. No one had bothered to say good-bye. Eventually she realized that no one had visited her in the night at all—there had never been a crowd of people coming here to her shipping container to seek refuge—and Josefina Guzman knew that she had dreamed them, the way old people dream of companionship and status. She spat derisively in the dirt. She felt ashamed of her vivid fantasies. She pinched herself many times on the arms, as penance.

Strangely though Father Juan del Rosario had left behind the giant Bible with the golden cover and the tall golden cross and the golden bowl from the sacristy. All of these golden things were tossed on the ground next to the stone that Father Juan Del Rosario had used as an altar.

And now—and soon in all of her memories of it as well—the stone was twelve feet wide and seven feet high. It stood far higher than her fingertips could reach, even if she stood on tiptoe, and the markings on it seemed to have changed.

Josefina Guzman still couldn't read what they said.

So she picked up the golden things and put them away for safekeeping.

She washed her face with water from her jug and she gathered some miner's lettuce and dandelions and boiled them in a pot and ate them.

She wished her dream bears would come again. She missed them.

She was tired, and she felt like napping, but she was afraid that instead of her bears and Woolly Mammoth she would dream of men wearing gas masks and so she stayed awake.

A raccoon came around later. She threw it an old piece of fishtail from her garbage pail, hoping it would stay and chat, but the raccoon caught the fishtail in mid-air and ran off with it and left her all alone again.

Book Six

The Land of Nethalem

Chapter Twenty-Eight
The Second Coming of Mary Mbwembwe

The next morning Mary Mbwembwe was miraculously cured. What's more she had become a splendid specimen of *panthera pardus*. "What am I to make of this new trial!" Mary Mbwembwe exclaimed when she discovered her new body. But then she took her situation in stride, and said: "I know of this phenomenon. Yes indeed." Her voice was shaking, but not too badly, considering. "I recall hearing in my childhood a story told by the people of my homeland, that we once possessed the knowledge to change ourselves into panthers by anointing our bodies with the blood of a newly slaughtered rooster. When in panther form we may do no harm to others, under pain of retaining forever the beast's shape."

"Yikes, Mary Mbwembwe is missing, and there's a black jaguar on the bed!" Stella said.

That is when Mary Mbwembwe realized that Stella couldn't understand her. In fact her pregnant friend was backing away while holding a chair in front of her like a lion tamer might, and the dogs were bristling and growling low in their throats. Only the house cat seemed unperturbed. Instead of backing away it leapt up onto the bed with Mary Mbwembwe and rubbed its face along Mary Mbwembwe's new whiskers.

"I believe this magnificent creature is in fact Mary Mbwembwe," Margie Peach said, and if Mary Mbwembwe could speak she would have shouted her thanks, but as it is she just nodded.

"Oh, heck, you're right!" Stella said, and dropped the chair. "I'm sorry, Mary Mbwembwe, I completely didn't recognize you."

Then Stella thought about the house cat in a new way.

She picked it up.

"Is that you, Bibi?" she whispered, and held her breath for the reply.

But the cat only looked bored and squirmed in her arms until Stella let it go.

"I'm not surprised that these cats have nothing to say for themselves," the chocolate-colored lab said authoritatively. "I believe only we dogs have come through the exposure to Agent-T while still retaining our innate human intelligence."

Mary Mbwembwe was not one to lose her temper so rather than springing upon the much weaker animal and tearing her to pieces she calmly picked up her headscarf from where it had fallen onto the floor and wound it around her head in the fashion she preferred.

"No, Doctor Queenie, I believe Mary Mbwembwe is still exactly herself," Margie Peach said. "Just because some of us may have a speech impediment, it does not mean we are less than the others."

Mary Mbwembwe nodded vigorously, and the matter was settled.

Now they were eager to get going. Once they left their hotel they discovered that the landscape all around had altered itself, with strange bushes and brambles growing over the cars and parking lots and highway overpasses and fast food places. The Marriott Hotel sign that had shone out like a bright red beacon only the night before was now completely covered over in kudzu. The look of the world had transformed overnight, from sidewalks and industrial parks and hospitals and hotels into something wild and rich and green.

And they did not know which way to go.

Then the Welsh Corgi yipped twice and told them she could smell the salt air from the bay.

After sniffing about for several minutes and conferring with one another, the other dogs agreed.

"Come on, guys," Stella said. "Let's go to Nethalem!"

Chapter Twenty-Nine

A Procession of Beasts

By this time in the story Stella could barely remember what Lix Tetrax looked like. Even so she felt drawn to Nethalem as one might be drawn to a favorite pop song drifting out from an open window, a comparison that sounded just right to Stella even if it happened that no pop song would drift out from an open window ever again. She hummed a little as they walked along. Her baby, inspired by her good mood, chimed in with its own little songs, first with a pitch-perfect rendition of "Bye-Bye Blackbird," and then with a sultry interpretation of "That Old Black Magic." Before too long the baby was caught up in the joyous expectation that they were nearing the end of their quest, and began to belt out a string of hits by Cannibal Corpse, one after another, starting with the band's iconic debut from the nineties, "Hammer Smashed Face."

Stella was distracted by her baby's singing and did not notice at first that animals of all shapes and sorts had begun to follow along, popping out of bushes or holes in the ground as the company passed.

"What the heck is going on with all these animals?" Stella said to Margie Peach, who seemed to know just about everything.

"Those over there are Manx Loaghtans," Margie Peach said, with authority, since systematic taxonomy was one of her many avocations. "And I see we also have some Lowland Streaked Tenrecs, and black-tailed deer, and some star moles. Since we started off this morning, I have counted four hundred and sixty-eight species of snake, two thousand and eighteen species of lizard, and six hundred and sixty-six varieties of arachnid. I believe I even caught sight of a passenger pigeon in the throng of birds above us, and I thought I saw a pig-footed bandicoot walking among the possums, but as these creatures are considered extinct I wonder if my eyes are deceiving me. The insects are too numerous and too peripatetic to count. Most of the birds are flying too high for my weak eyesight to make a foolproof identification. They might all be former people. They might be *bona fide* animals. Whatever the truth is I'm overcome with emotion to see them. I know what they are feeling. You have drawn them here, Stella—you, and the child you carry in your womb."

Her dog-friend's theory sounded unlikely, but Stella didn't argue. All kinds of animals were shuffling and loping along with them and the herd kept getting larger and louder and more smelly, and the sky above was so full of birds that it looked like an upside-down ocean covered in the white-tipped waves of many wings. Owls were flying in long ribbons, and red-tail hawks and golden eagles did tricks in the air, and sea birds were screeching and diving, and in between these larger birds flew the starlings and sparrows and swallows, tracing startled patterns that looked like smoke with a mind of its own.

There weren't any people besides Stella and her baby, though. Stella began to wonder whether there were any other humans left on the planet. Of course it was a silly idea. Even so she felt like Adam.

Margie Peach thought it was her job, as a dog, to remain upbeat, and so she did not share with Stella any of her misgivings about the throng of animals that had joined them. Margie had lived her life trying her best not to judge others harshly—after all, she knew firsthand what it was like to be a unfairly judged by others—but she had to admit that some of the animals slithering and skulking along with them were less than good company. She could have done without the order *arachnida* altogether, and neither *rodentia* nor *squamata* had ever been favorites of hers. She hoped at least that the creatures that were sneaking and skittering among them now were actual snakes and spiders and rats by birth, and that they were not humans transformed by Agent-T. She couldn't imagine what it would be like to discover you were a literal rat or snake or spider, and she counted herself lucky, not for the last time, to have become a dog.

This line of thinking led her to contemplate whether fate was fair, and all sorts of other theological matters. She began to wonder, for instance, if people became nasty creatures or noble creatures because of the way they had lived their lives as human beings. There was no way of knowing, though, because other than her pack, and Stella herself, none of the creatures seemed capable of coherent speech.

As she trotted along, Margie Peach next began to worry what would happen when the meat-eaters got hungry. She got the shivers whenever she thought of that rabbit being carried off in a German Shepherd's jaws.

She fell in with the Doberman, whom Margie recalled had once been a preacher.

"I feel no interest in eating meat," Margie Peach said. "Do you have a similar feeling, I wonder?"

The Doberman nodded. "I too have lost my appetite for the flesh," she said. "I could be perfectly happy eating grass. '*The wolf shall dwell with the lamb, and the leopard shall lie down with the kid; and the calf* and the young lion and the fatling together; and a little child shall lead them."*

"I've heard that before," Margie Peach said.

"I often chose it for my sermons," the Doberman said. "Even the children could relate to it."

Margie Peach nodded.

"You know so much about so many things," she said. "I have wondered whether you might have any theories about what's happening to us. You have to admit, it's a little apocryphal."

"There are so many Biblical stories of animals talking," the Doberman said. "The serpent, for instance, is a famous talker. I would not be surprised if one of these snakes pipes up eventually, and begins a conversation with us. There is also the story of Balaam's ass, in the Book of Numbers, who tells Balaam, '*Am not I thine ass, Balaam, upon which thou hast ridden ever since I was thine, unto this day?*'"

"You would think that if a man called Balaam had an ass that could talk he would have written down every word it ever said and not just this one small thing of no consequence," Margie Peach said.

The Doberman growled a little.

"Well, all right," Margie said. "Does the Bible give any tips about what we should expect next?"

"No doubt the most pertinent passages for our situation are in the Book of Revelation," the Doberman said, full of pride, and she proved her mastery of the Word by reciting: *There was a woman who was pregnant and cried out with pain because she was about to give birth. There was a giant Beast with seven heads and ten horns that wanted to eat the woman's baby as soon as it was born.*

The Doberman spoke magisterially. The majesty of the biblical passage had seized her soul and had left her feeling rapturous.

"That sounds terrible," Margie Peach said. "What kind of religion predicts baby-eating by a giant Beast?"

"Don't worry, it's a metaphor," the Doberman said, her tongue lolling. "The woman represents the Old Testament. The baby is Jesus."

The Doberman's glittering certitude about such a wicked story unnerved Margie Peach, and she dropped back and began walking instead alongside the chocolate-colored lab.

"You know what, Margie Peach? I wouldn't be surprised if I could teach all of these animals to speak eventually," the chocolate-colored lab said, exactly as if they had been chatting about just this subject for some time. "I'm a healer at heart. My background is in speech pathology. In my former life I was very skilled at teaching speech to patients after they had lost their larynx."

"I'm glad you think animals besides us dogs might be able to speak eventually," Margie Peach said. She was filled with quiet satisfaction to hear the doctor speak so optimistically about the future, especially since the lab had been so despondent about her prospects in those first early days.

Just then a huge bird separated from the flocking birds above and came diving toward them and shrieked: WOE! WOE! WOE!

The bird's cries sounded tantalizingly like language to them both, and after the giant bird flew back up into the air they were left feeling amazed and hopeful that one day all the good creatures of the earth would understand one another perfectly.

Chapter Thirty
A Crow Comes to Josefina Guzman

Now our story turns back to the crow who was once an old woman trying to make a fast buck off of the Apocalypse by charging refugees five dollars a mile.

We return to the very first moment when the door of the truck is flung open by a man with broken glasses.

The crow flies out and startles the man.

The man reacts by grabbing a gun and shooting a woman wearing a white turban, and the woman falls to the ground.

The crow doesn't linger or even think twice about this tragedy. She is a crow. She flies up into the night sky, no longer concerned with guns or money or people. She flies toward the stars, where she joins a tumult of other birds in a flock so thick and crowded that she (inexperienced with the art of flying in formation) is tumbled about and battered by the bigger birds: the gulls, the owls, the eagles, the falcons. She is terrified until she understands, in a flash of instinct that is common with birds, that these other birds were once people, too.

She remembers she is an old woman who can't fly.

She tumbles earthward.

She recovers and ascends again, too filled with wonder to do otherwise, and flies along to the rhythm of her wingbeats with no other thought than the craving for this sky; this night; this movement west.

As she beats on, steady now, she becomes aware of all that is absent from her life. She lists the absences one by one, in her crow's mind, because crows can count. The absence of arthritis; the absence of myopia; the absence of eczema; the absence of loneliness—the obliteration of solitude, because the crow finds herself flying together with hundreds, thousands of other birds—and she has found the winged memory and rhythm of her species now, the beat, beat, beat, and just see how strong her arms her wings have become!

She sees Angels flying among them, searching urgently for someone on the ground—a girl, maybe—but the crow and all the other birds spread out like a thick dark blanket over the world and hide the girl, and the Angels fly back up to Heaven, defeated.

She sees the dark world below.

She sees flashes of lightning and hears rumblings, peals of thunder.

She sees warring armies clash on each of the seven continents, rushing toward their mutually assured destruction, only to abandon their armaments in the field—what use are armaments when the warriors have no arms?—and she sees the former soldiers, now animals, gallop off, or fly away, or fight on with nothing more than tooth and claw.

She sees a great city split in three parts.

Sun and moon stand still in their lofty abode.

She sees hailstones fall from the sky, so huge and slow that she and the other birds can fly around them easily, or even perch upon them as they fall.

She feels a pull toward a new direction and banks away from the circling throng, and flies down to the ground, where she finds herself looking into the kindly face of a small, dry, weather-beaten, almost-beautiful woman, with seagull feathers in her hair.

Chapter Thirty-One

Josefina Guzman Rescues Wanda Lubiejewski from Her Wandering

A crow flew down and settled on Josefina Guzman's shoulder as she made her way down the dirt path through the weeds and reeds.

"Well, there you are," Josefina Guzman said. "You could have let me know you were coming."

Josefina Guzman was on her way to the village of Nethalem, to complain to Father Juan del Rosario about his inopportune visit the night before with his rag-tag band of pretend refugees. She would check with him first to see if he had come at all, of course, and if he had, then she planned to give him a good talking-to.

The village of Nethalem looked like a ghost town.

A pale indeterminate darkness fell like perpetual silver moonlight sifting down from the sky. The houses glinted. Some had burned down. A charred ruined scent hung in the air. There was no sound of television sets carrying on the wind through the windows. Nobody was in a driveway leaning over an open-hood truck, looking for a reason why the engine wouldn't start. No smell of menudo being cooked on the stoves. No ice cream truck. No grandmothers watching their grandchildren play in scrubbed-neat front yards.

No airplanes overhead.

A strong scent of ash and smoke and sadness.

A peculiar silence.

But not an utter silence: birds twittered in the trees, lots of them, bending down the branches with their collective weight and singing out in the odd twilight. Dogs were knocking over trashcans and rooting through their contents, tails wagging. Roosters screeched. Four sheep were grazing on the weeds in front of the rectory. The rectory door was open. Josefina Guzman knocked on the open door. When no one answered she walked in.

"Father?" she called. "Father Juan del Rosario?"

No one.

The crow crowed.

"You're right," Josefina Guzman said to the crow. "These are not normal times at all."

She tried the light switch because it was dim and a little scary inside. But the electricity was out. She walked down the narrow dim hallway with her fingers touching the wall, to guide her, until she came to the room where not so many days ago she had watched a news story about a confused white rhinoceros.

"Hello? Hello?" she said.

Nobody answered.

Feeling more burglar than parishioner, Josefina Guzman went out into the street again.

"Hello? Hello?" she called. "Is there anyone? Anyone at all?"

No one.

So Josefina Guzman decided to walk all the way to the big city, seven miles down the road. She was bound to run into someone along the way. Someone who would explain everything, so she could go back home knowing that nothing had changed, and that her pleasant-enough life could go on happily until the end.

A scent she couldn't name was drifting in the air, and it was growing stronger and more mysterious with each step—not wood smoke, but something deeper, and older. Josefina Guzman was not afraid. She was used to the idea of mortal danger coming for her with every breath. All of her sisters and brothers had died in their fifties and she was living on borrowed time.

The crow, an old friend by now, kept her company as she walked. Sometimes it perched on her shoulder, and sometimes on her head, and sometimes it hopped alongside or made small flights hither and thither when something bright caught its eye. The crow would always give the prize to Josefina Guzman. The crow presented her with a silver Uno Bar wrapper, and a California Highway Patrol badge, and many bullet casings of various gauges. Josefina Guzman thanked the crow each time, and deposited each offering into her deep pockets and went on.

She came to the road that led out from the village of Nethalem, and followed it for a mile, until she got to the eight-lane road that commuters used to bypass her part of the world. On this day the road was choked with abandoned cars. Cars were willy-nilly skewed across the lanes, their doors ajar. Old rustbuckets and pickup trucks and service vans were mixed in with Mercedes Benzes and Cadillacs, all tumbled together, some upside-down, and with their keys still dangling in the locks. She didn't touch anything. She didn't want to look inside the trunks. She began to wonder just how far the loneliness went. To the ends of the earth? To the next street over? She didn't know. "I just don't know, I just don't know," she said aloud, and her words echoed back to her in the hard and brittle silence, and she resolved not to say anything else for the moment.

The crow was still with her. She whistled to it as it hopped and fluttered from one empty car to the next, and it cawed lovingly in reply.

That was when Josefina Guzman heard a voice, thin and plaintive in the shimmer of silence that surrounded her. She walked toward the voice eagerly. It seemed to be getting more solemn and more melancholy as she drew near, and when she got there, she saw the voice came from a radio left on in a car, and the battery was running down. She closed the car door and walked on.

After a while she found herself walking in an endless prairie of office buildings. All the windows were broken. Then she came to a high fence with an enormous sign that said GREAT AMERICA on it. She saw it was a theme park. Pennants drooped on the tall flagpoles. Silent rollercoasters rose up like ancient ruins.

Three blocks later she startled a flock of pigeons and they flew up with a raucous flapping of wings. Josefina Guzman's crow joined them, and circled with them. The crow looked exactly like a stark black crow's eye in a gray-feathered body, and Josefina Guzman knew the crow was going to fly off with the pigeons. Her solitude expanded, as did her sorrow. The crow was going to abandon her to be with its own kind, and then she really would be alone.

But her crow came back. Josefina Guzman was so happy that her crow came back that she forgot to be sad or worried, and walked forward with the heart of a child. And then it seemed to Josefina Guzman that the scene all around her, which had just moments ago seemed so stark, so dead, so free of all movement and life, was in fact full of life. She saw a spring-green furze growing up the sides of the buildings and across the roads and over the tires of the cars; and in this mat of green life, mossy and rich, she became aware, in that startled way that can sometimes happen when you have been looking at something a long time before really seeing it, that there were frogs and salamanders and other living things perched in it, small animals of such glorious color and variety and abundance that she couldn't understand why she didn't see them before. She had been so busy noticing all that what was missing: the people, the traffic, the sirens—that she hadn't noticed at first how noisy and full of life her surroundings had become. The creatures sang in chirrups and croaks. Now and then a grander base tone would come and Josefina Guzman would spot a bullfrog that had found a luminous puddle to claim as its own. As she walked on, the salamanders and frogs gave way to larger things. She saw burrowing owls and squirrels. She saw small earless creatures that moved in packs like dogs, but that were not dogs. She saw cats, too, loping at the edges—bobcat, house cat, lynx. A wave of parrots flew up from a rooftop like a living flag and circled and flew away.

The buildings got taller. In the midst of the abandoned cars she saw an occasional army truck. She walked past a tank that was tilted at a crazy angle and half up on a sidewalk. Gradually the civilian cars thinned out and the military vehicles grew more frequent until the streets were jammed with an invading army's worth of tanks and trucks. Guns of all sorts were lying in the street. She kept tripping over them. She picked one up and felt the weight of it and decided it was not for her and put it down again.

She saw a stately movement on the next street down and thought: "It's a giraffe."

The giraffe came toward her. It swayed its neck in questioning undulations. It bent down and looked straight into her eyes, and she felt blessed.

"Oh, glorious creature," she thought; "your eyes feel familiar to me. You are so sad." But she wasn't the one the giraffe was looking for. It gazed at her sadly, and then it began a stately retreat, all alone again, and Josefina Guzman felt sorry for it.

She heard a sigh behind her: a deep low breath, almost lower than sound itself. She turned around.

She saw her very own two bears from her dream.

She hadn't known from her dream, though, that her bears would be as big as monuments.

"So we finally meet," she said.

The bears nodded their great heads. They came close, bent low. The bears were happy to see her. They were happy to see the crow too. The air between Josefina Guzman and the bears and the crow was humming; it was singing. She wasn't sure if what was happening to her was real, or a dream, or dementia, or death, or if in fact it was

171

none of these things. The bears enveloped her in their warmth and welcome, and she knew in spite of all her doubts and worries that she was meant to have found them.

"Come along, bears, let's go home," Josefina Guzman said.

Chapter Thirty-Two
Why the Condor was Late

The President was sick. Bedridden. The President's ruddy skin had developed a killer case of the shingles, and his luxuriant-red, flowing, lustrous, virile, and Samson-like hair, once the envy of all others, was coming out in clumps. Hair furred his pillow each morning. Major Eureka Yamanaka did her best to tend to him. When he could no longer eat solids she fed him liquids through a straw. She had never liked him and she felt besieged now by his bellicose insistence that now was the time, if ever, to "bring out the nukes."

She didn't trust her memories of the events that led them to this state of abandonment from loyal troops and career professionals alike. She remembers shouts, and gunfire. As she ran toward the commotion, her own gun at the ready to defend her country, she had been met with a sea of small furry creatures running in the opposite direction: lemming, mink, ferret, otter; their fur rippling and their bodies undulating in a mass of life and purpose: to get somewhere else; to escape. A fleeing panic. She tried to find her lover in the mob and failed. The underground Command Center, however impregnable to nuclear attack, was not meant to hold creatures like these. They squeezed through vents. They ran through pipes. Before long there were only a few errant left-behinds squealing in the corners. Feeling pity, she put out bowls of water for them. They lapped it up once she backed away.

She brought the President water, too.

She bathed his inflamed skin.

She felt the gathering urge to be elsewhere and pored over the Command Center's topographical maps with a need to discover where she was supposed to be, until one day, accidentally, her eyes fell on a tiny dot on a map of northern California, and she discovered the place where she was meant to be was called *Nethalem*.

She yearned for it.

She tended to the President, loyal to her oath.

"I feel sick," the President said. "I feel very, very sick."

The President had taken a turn for the worse that day. The scaling on his skin had grown into thick fungal ridges that encased his arms and legs and made their way up over his neck and across his face. The last strands of his once-luxuriant-red, flowing, lustrous, virile, and Samson-like hair had finally fallen out completely. His bare scalp was spottled. His breaths came in huffed snorts. Before today he had been able to get up from bed and to make his way to the toilet, or to wash himself on his own, but now these routines were beyond him. He smelled terrible. He was suffering. The rest of the world had abandoned him. She was the last soldier standing.

"Sit here, closer, just sit with me," he said.

There was a chair next to his bed. She sat with him. He was freakishly transformed but still somehow exactly himself. If there had been more time maybe someone could have come up with an antidote for them all. But there had not been enough time. The medical team had run off into the pipes and ducts with the rest of them. Day by day she had watched her own body change. Her hands scaled over and her fingers grew into something a little more like talons. She had seen enough feeds from the drones to know that she was destined to become some kind of predatory bird. The President, though—he was an unknown. She did not recognize his type at all. His spine stretched and arched and twisted. Now and then he let out a voluminous bellow.

"We're the only two left," he said. "Like Adam and Eve."

His chest heaved from the effort to speak and she pitied him.

"If it had been up to me I would never have picked an Oriental," the President said. "I've never been attracted to Oriental women. No shape at all. Hell, Hell, Hell."

These last words were followed by a bout of asthmatic wheezes.

Something was happening under the sheets—a mound was growing, there at the center.

Major Eureka Yamanaka stood. She drew her weapon.

"I feel sick," the President said.

With a sudden muscular recovery he sprang from the bed and tried to grab her in the coarsest way possible. She stepped back. She fired her weapon. When he didn't stop she fired the whole clip into him. She saw the bullets sink into his bare chest, just barely, and there they stuck, as if they were peppering an impregnable shell.

The President sprouted new heads.

He came toward her with claws groping.

Major Eureka Yamanaka ran.

She forced herself to think coldly about how to defend herself. As she ran her wings began to form and she was not surprised. She heard thunderous crashing from behind her and knew he had broken through a doorframe that he had grown too large to pass through; that he had broken through concrete reinforcements; that he was coming. She ran down the corridor and into the cavernous Command Room. The monitors were all black. The chairs were all empty. The giant screen on the front wall was blank. Guns and notebooks and pens and animal droppings were scattered all over the floor. When she reached the armory she grabbed an M16 rifle with her talons and turned to make her stand. The President came on. She fired at him until her magazine was empty, and still he came, the wattle of his throat wobbling. His arms reached out. His heads bobbled and danced.

The earth shook.

And the floor, seemingly so impregnable, began to crack, at first slowly, and then gaining speed and force until a jagged-zipper yawn of a hole opened up in the floor.

The hole expanded in seconds and the two of them suddenly stood on opposite sides of an un-leap-able chasm, separated by thirty yards or more.

They stared at one another.

She saw him gauging the distance, ready to test his new legs, deciding he could make it.

He smiled at her. He was coming for her.

The floor lurched.

The President fell in.

The President opened all seven mouths and screamed.

It was not a scream of despair—no: it was a seven-throated scream of triumph, a guttural cry that sounded like: "I won! I won! I won!"

And with that, the President turned upside-down, and with all seven heads pointing straight into the pit, he dove straight down and disappeared.

The air was still.

The President was gone.

Sunlight and fresh air drifted down to Major Eureka Yamanaka from a jagged gap that had opened in the ceiling.

She felt an overwhelming desire to test her wings.

But first she hovered above the pit, to make sure the danger had passed.

She held herself aloft, no longer surprised at anything, and looked down.

She did not see any sign of the President.

Her job here was done.

Major Eureka Yamanaka lifted herself skyward and drifted through the broad sunlit gap in the ceiling. The blue sky beckoned, and the air was sweet. She knew where she was going, and she knew that she was late. She banked on a crosscurrent and flew with all her strength toward Nethalem.

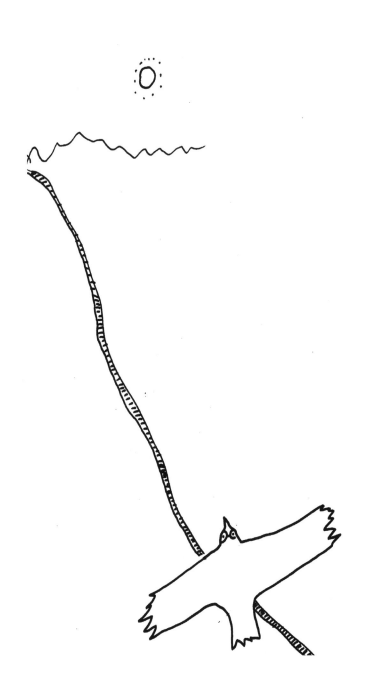

Chapter Thirty-Three
Take Away the Stone

The two bears followed Josefina Guzman as she made her way home to Nethalem, just as she knew they would. Now and then they would nuzzle her and breathe their bearish breath over her, enveloping her in a cloud of deep-musk affection. But it was the crow who was most affectionate of all, rarely leaving her shoulder and caressing her neck with its soft breast underfeathers as they walked home.

On the way back she gathered provisions. From a market she took two loaves of bread and a bag of dinner rolls and a brick of cheese and six apples and a bottle of red wine. The crow indicated that she was very fond of raisins, and so Josefina Guzman took many boxes of them from the shelf and added them to her cart. She took two large steaks from the cold storage locker, too, for the bears. Although the power was out, the meat was still cold, and it smelled fresh. When she was satisfied with what she had gathered, she found a notepad and pen by the cash register and wrote: *I have taken items in the amount of $107.18 and I have not accounted for tax, if any. Please forgive. I will repay when able.* The bears had waited in the parking lot. The smaller bear was playing with the shopping carts, getting them to roll along with a bright shove of its snout and then laughing when it crashed into the other carts. She offered the other bear a steak. But the bear turned away from the meat. Josefina Guzman offered an apple next, and the bear ate it. The smaller bear came over and she offered it the meat, but this bear, too, wanted apples. The bears ate all six of the apples, three each, taking the fruit from her hand discreetly with their lips. After they ate all the apples they looked at her expectantly. She offered them bread and they ate it delicately, barely making crumbs.

Josefina Guzman went back into the store and found two ten-pound bags of apples and sixteen loaves of bread and put them in a cart. She also took two gallon-cans of honey, and another three bricks of cheese. On the way out she took a fifth of tequila. Although she was not a big drinker it felt like she might want fortification in the days to come. She amended the note to the storeowner to account for her new purchases and went out.

"That's all I can push in this cart, for now," she told the bears. "We can come back for more another day."

The walk home seemed longer than the journey out. The bears seemed to intuit her fatigue. The larger one took her gently in its jaws and carried her, and as it did so it hummed softly to reassure her that its intentions were peaceful and loving. The younger bear did a remarkable job pushing the cart of groceries along, with its snout. The crow fluttered close by, cooing and fanning her face lovingly. She heard shuffles, squeals, and groans coming from the dusk in all directions, but these did not alarm her. It felt so good to be going home, and with friends. When they got back to her clearing, her shipping container looked like it had been waiting for her. She was not surprised to discover that the white stone had grown ever more enormous.

The larger bear put Josefina Guzman down gently and walked up to the stone and leaned its head on it, one ear pressed to its surface, as if listening. The smaller bear did too.

The crow flew up from Josefina Guzman's shoulder and perched on top of the stone, cocking its head to look from one bear to the next. The three animals seemed to be deep in conversation. Josefina Guzman felt left out.

"What is it, you rascals?" she said grumpily, and the three of them looked at her, and she felt a shimmer of a thought coming out of them—not disapproval, exactly, but the vivid sense that she had interrupted important work. They turned back to their conversation.

Then both bears leaned their meaty shoulders against the stone and hummed low in their throats, and pushed. Their feet dug in. The crow flew up from the stone and hovered above as if worried its weight would impede the bears. It cawed in encouragement.

Howmmmm, the bears hummed.

They were trying to move the stone.

Of course they were.

Instantly Josefina Guzman felt the same strong urge, to move the stone. The urge was undeniable. The stone must be moved.

"Somehow this stone is demanding to be moved," Josefina Guzman said to the bears. "Look here, you bears, can I help?"

The bears nodded with vigor.

Josephina Guzman scrambled in between the two of them. She put her own stringy shoulder to the side of the stone. When the bears pushed, she pushed, with all her might. The crow above cackled its encouragement. The stone did not move. "How old I have become!" Josefina Guzman cried inside. "I am nothing but a dry bit of loose string. I am a crumpled scrap of paper. I have no strength in me." But the bears did not nudge her away. They did not forbid her to help them or tell her to go sit to one side like a useless old woman. When the bears breathed in, Josefina Guzman breathed in; and when the bears roared, she roared, and put her scrap-paper shoulder to the side of the stone and pushed. She willed the stone to dislodge from its place. As she pushed her left ear came naturally in contact with the stone. To her surprise the stone was warm, not cool, not the way you expected a stone to feel, and it rippled across her cheek like a muscle, not the way you would expect a stone to behave at all. Now that her ear was pressed against the stone she could hear it pulsing like heartbeat, deep inside. Something needed to give. Something needed to get out. Something needed to be released. The bears breathed in and Josefina

183

Guzman breathed in and then they shouted out an ecstatic breath and pushed, together.

No dice. It didn't budge.

A feeling came over Josefina Guzman. "Is it my Heart?" she thought. "Has it come to this, that my Heart is breaking?" Then her jaw began to hurt as if she had sixteen toothaches at once, and her ears began to ring. She grew very hot. And then all these unpleasant feelings went away and instead she felt very strong, very good. How rich and strong to feel horns sprouting from her head! How glossy her coat, and how considerably grateful she felt, to be a goat!

The other bears licked her face. Then they retreated. They gave her a moment.

"Did that just really happen to me?" she said.

She accepted it.

The bears came back. They put their shoulders to the mass of stone. They breathed in and then let out roars that shook the ground. The stone complained. It groaned and screeched. Slowly, slowly, it began to budge. Or did it? Maybe it was only Josefina Guzman's wishful thinking.

They stopped trying.

They panted and slumped.

And when they tried again every cell and thought inside them willed the stone to move, and they pushed like they never pushed before, until they felt their hearts threaten to rip right out from their chests, and Josefina Guzman felt an ecstatic urge welling up inside her to make a running start and to lower her head and to go rushing toward the stone and butt it—

And the stone rolled away.

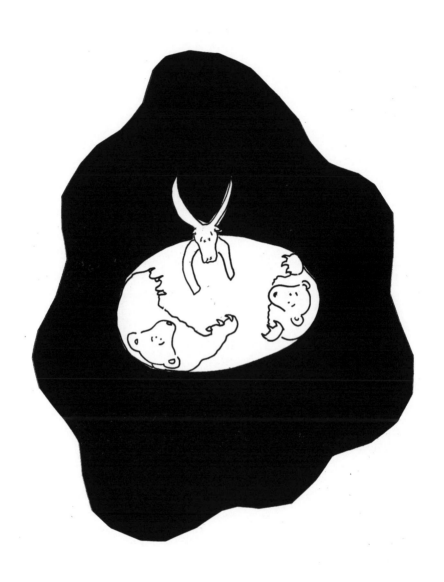

Chapter Thirty-Four
The Coming of the Beast

Josefina Guzman opened her eyes.

She was lying on a knob of grass and mud by the side of her clearing, a good thirty feet away from the stone. Her four hooves were in the air. She had been thrown clear as the stone had rolled away, as if she and the bears had released some explosive force that had belched its way to the surface. Now her crow was fanning her with soft warm wingbeats, and hovering above her face, and looking into her eyes with loving concern.

"Thank you dear," she said to the crow. "I'm all right. No harm done."

The crow looked relieved. It laughed and nodded. Meanwhile the two bears were waking up on the other side of the clearing, flung far from the stone, like her, and they were shaking their shaggy heads, stunned and amazed at whatever force had thrown them so far.

Josefina Guzman and the bears and the crow made their cautious way over to where the stone had once rested.

To their wonder they saw a deep pit where the stone used to be.

They leaned over as far as they dared and looked in. The pit went straight down, as far as they could see, until all light had been used up and all that was left was a black spot, unknowable, a perfectly round hole of a void, traveling straight down into the depths of dark.

A few birds fluttered overhead.

Then many more birds.

Then so many birds that the sun was blotted out and a thunderous noise filled the air and Josefina Guzman felt the ground shake as if from the boots of an army on the march.

A pregnant girl flung herself into the clearing from the reeds.

"Hey, a goat! Wow, look at these giant bears!" said the pregnant girl. "Does anybody around here know a guy named Lix Tetrax?"

Before Josefina Guzman could answer—whether with words or a bleat she couldn't say—the pregnant girl saw the pit and walked straight to the edge of it.

"Will you look at that," the pregnant girl said.

She got on her knees and stared down.

They all followed her to the edge and stared down into the pit, except for Josefina Guzman, because she was instead looking around with wonder at the creatures in her clearing. They each seemed so glorious and strong, and she was one of them. She felt young again.

And here was the girl Josefina Guzman had dreamed about, such a pregnant girl, her hair matted and wild, and she was wearing nothing more than a hospital gown covered in smiley-suns, tied in back with two strings and with her bare bottom sassily showing. The girl was laughing in tremendous snorts, as if reliving some very funny event. Josefina Guzman laughed too, in a goat-like way, and all of the creatures, hundreds or thousands or hundreds of thousands of them, some with remnants of clothes from their past lives but mostly buck-naked, began to screech and to stomp their feet in a celebratory way that made them feel closer to one another no matter what their species. Josefina Guzman felt amazed and proud to be part of their company, although she also felt shy to have such thoughts, and full of self-deprecating doubt, because she had always been a nobody, and now she was a goat.

"Margie Peach, I feel somehow this goat and these bears are important, and that I'm important, too, and you are important, and Mary Mbwembwe is important," the pregnant girl said. "I feel like we're meant to fit together like puzzle pieces. I think something is about to happen, and that we're stuck in the middle of it, and what we do next will have consequences until the end of all time."

It thrilled Josefina Guzman to hear her thoughts spoken aloud by the pregnant girl. She wished she could do more than bleat her agreement.

Just then a fragrant, delectable wind began to rise out of the pit, distracting her.

Josefina Guzman and the other animals edged and crowded toward the pit, looking in, trying to imagine what had caused such a scent.

The black eye of the pit looked up at Josefina Guzman.

Josefina Guzman discovered that she was no longer completely happy, because that black eye staring at her from the depths of the pit looked like a malevolent eye, and its gaze looked so hypnotic and evil that Josefina Guzman might have fallen in if a black chow had not pulled her back by her stumpy tail.

There was something down there.

Something that did not belong.

They could all feel it.

The air grew cold and frost crackled near the edge of the pit and killed the first green things near it.

A sound came rising up out of the pit, as if from an eternal earth-horn, blasting the lowest bass note ever sounded.

The sound made their animal ears ring, and they cried out, each in their own way.

Out of the pit fell the Beast.

"Lix Tetrax? Is that you?" the girl said.

Chapter Thirty-Five
Kitchen Shears

"Hello, baby," one of the heads said. "You got here just in time."

The other heads screeched and barked and preened in many directions, snakily, scanning the crowd, confusing them, until one of the eyes settled again on Stella, and all seven heads came toward the girl, entwining, examining, huffing out with a craven old-person sensuality through huge smelly nostrils. None of the animals could quite figure out why this Beast felt so familiar to them, until the Beast stood up vainly on two legs, as if to terrorize them all with the size of his monster-sized cock and his globular, pustulant balls hanging in their gizzardy sacs, and all at once Margie Peach knew exactly who the Beast reminded her of.

"It's the President!" the young beagle barked.

And Stella saw that it was true: that the charismatic Lix Tetrax was merely another face of the President, who was just another face of this Beast; and she had been taken in by his slimy charms, and she had made excuses for him, and she had blamed herself when he behaved badly, and only now was his true nature revealed to her, as he spittled and spat, and as his blistery skin glistened in the heat of a sun that looked far too close and too big.

AND THE MONSTER STOOD IN FRONT OF THE WOMAN WHO WAS ABOUT TO GIVE BIRTH SO THAT IT MIGHT DEVOUR HER CHILD THE MOMENT HE WAS BORN, her baby cried joyfully.

"Oh, heck," Stella said.

"What are you waiting for?" the Beast shouted magisterially. "Don't you know you are my Creatures, the Soulless and the Forgotten

Ones, the Lost, the Damned, the Deplorable Sluts, the Carnal Fallen, the Whores and the Sinners? Worship me! Fight for me! Together we will defeat all who are stupid enough to challenge us!" And the Beast roared in ecstasy from all seven mouths at once.

Without hesitation the snakes and the rats and the stoats and the  bats and all the other evil creatures ran and flew to him, and swarmed up his tree-like legs, and scurried through his fur, all over his body, and covered him with tiny welcome kisses and nibbles, while the other animals ran away in terror to hide in the reeds.

And just a handful of sad, small creatures found themselves standing alone against the Beast: one goat, a dog with her pack, two bears, a black panther, a crow, and a pregnant girl.

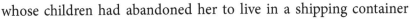

They fell to the ground with their ears ringing and their souls crushed.

"It's true, I'm nothing and no one without this Beast," Josefina Guzman thought, because she remembered that she was an old woman who bathed too infrequently and whose children had abandoned her to live in a shipping container  that had come to rest on top of an industrial waste dump next to a sewage treatment plant, and also, that she was a goat.

"It's no use," thought Margie Peach, and reminded herself that the natural fate of all animals was to be eaten alive; and she was filled with despair, and remembered how she had been mocked for her disability her whole life and that no one had ever wanted to hear anything about her whip-tail lizards, not even her own mother.

"We are doomed," thought Wanda Lubiejewski, and remembered that no man had ever in her life looked her in the eye, or thought of her as a person, because they were distracted by her size M breasts ever since she was twelve.

"I give up," Mary Mbwembwe thought, because she remembered she was an illegal with no family and no home, and that she had spent her life emptying the bedpans of old people who did not remember her from one day to the next, and that she was now a smelly black panther with no way to speak up for herself.

"You mean we're the bad guys?" Stella said.

"What do you think?" the head of Lix Tetrax roared. "Of course you're bad! You're an unwed pregnant teen! How is the little Antichrist, hmm?"

EGO SUM DOMINUS PESTIFER MUNDI her baby shouted joyfully.

Stella went into labor.

That first contraction knocked all the punch out of her.

Then the contraction was over.

Stella took a breath.

She stood as tall as she could under the circumstances.

She remembered that Lix Tetrax couldn't tell her what to do. Not now. Not ever. "Come on, dogs!" Stella yelled. "Come on, bears and goat! Come on, Mary Mbwembwe! We can beat this old loser!"

"It's no good," the goat said. "What help can I be? I'm made in Satan's own image."

But the panther Mary Mbwembwe, who was an Animist and therefore did not believe in the Devil, took her place next to Stella and began to stamp upon the ground with her paws and to rumble righteous anger in her throat.

Next Margie Peach, gaining courage from Mary Mbwembwe's example, took up the rhythm of the doomed panther and stamped on the ground in time.

And then the other dogs, and the bears, and finally the goat herself began to stamp on the ground in a rousing and united way, until they all felt like Zulu warriors, who, at the famous battle of kwaJimu, had stood together on the last hill at sunset, before the battle, and had stamped on the ground with their spears, and had sung a triumphant battle song together, and had rushed forward courageously, only to be slaughtered by a vastly more powerful enemy.

The Beast snarled and laughed and the snakes and rats all hissed and bared their fangs from within the Beast's fur. Trees uprooted themselves. Thunder and fire fell upon the face of the deep.

"You don't belong on Earth at all!" the Doberman cried bravely. "Go back to Heaven from whence you came, you old Deceiver!"

The Beast spat from its seven gullets and took a monster-step forward toward the tiny group of resisters, his feet ready to squash them, and his claws ready to scoop them up and tear them apart, or maybe eat them for breakfast—

And that is when a Great Woolly Mammoth came out of nowhere and rushed fearlessly and righteously and without hesitation toward the Enemy.

The Beast slapped the Great Woolly Mammoth sideways and the poor creature sailed without complaint through the air and fell to the ground, dead.

Stella and her friends stared at the Great Woolly Mammoth's carcass.

They charged.

The Welsh Corgi ran ahead, leaping and dodging, and she made a mighty leap onto the Beast's Achilles heel, as if this task alone was what she was born for, and she clamped down her jaws and would not be shaken off. Seeing the Corgi's bravery, the beagle leapt up next to her, and the two dogs held on like pennants flapping. Margie Peach and the Doberman and the chocolate-colored lab and the bears and the goat ran in circles to confuse the beast, while Stella grabbed onto one of the monster's furry hooves, and held on. She began to climb the Beast's leg, clenching her handy kitchen shears between her teeth as she grabbed tufts of the creature's rank fur. The Beast shook and stomped. Stella hung on. High above she could see Mary Mbwembwe already making her way toward one of the Beast's mottled throats to rip it out. She could see the bears and the goat attacking from the ground below. She saw other animals—other dogs, and wolves, coyotes, birds, a giraffe—had joined their side and were fighting alongside them, and against the Beast, and she rejoiced. She climbed up, up, grabbing the fur and clinging fast with her fingers and toes.

"Fat losers!" the Beast bellowed. "I'm your legitimate Leader! You're supposed to worship me!"

Stella's next contraction came. She gripped the Beast's fur, hanging on. The contraction passed. She climbed higher. Her arms were weary. Bees and rats leapt from Beast's matted hairs, stinging her fingers and

"Stella climbed, up, up, grabbing the fur and clinging fast with her fingers and toes."

nipping at her feet. She doubted herself. She was no hero. "Witch Hunt!" the Beast bellowed. In a frenzy he began to attack his own allies. Animal bodies were torn in half. Birds lay in bleeding heaps.

So far the Beast hadn't felt Stella as she made her way up his noxious leg. She could sense him searching for her in the tumult below, and searching for the baby too.

And then a muscle of the monster's leg contracted beneath her, and she knew that the Beast had felt her clinging to his sticky fur.

A vast dark shadow fell over her as one of the heads swung in her direction.

Stella closed her eyes and waited for the end to come.

But the eye that turned in Stella's direction looked like hot tapioca, because just seconds earlier it had been slashed to pudding by the California Condor once known as Major Eureka Yamanaka, who had arrived just in time.

The Beast did not see Stella.

The head moved off.

"We're going to make it, baby," Stella whispered, exuberant now, because at last she felt that fate was on their side, no matter what the Bible had to say about it.

Moments later Stella's jubilation was crushed when Mary Mbwembwe came falling past, silently and sadly and slowly, and only inches away, flung from on high by the swipe of a claw; and in the wafer-thin slice of time when the two of them were exactly at eye-level they nodded to one another, in the tacit understanding that they had done their best, and that they had lost. Then Mary Mbwembe continued on, down and down, to disappear from Stella's sight in the tumult below.

And seeing the multitudes so far below, fighting and hating and killing one another on account of this Beast, Stella felt a hot-to-the-core righteous fury flare up in her; and in the very moment when all hope was lost, she made a mighty, hopeless leap from the Beast's leg onto his ball sac, and she clung there with all her strength and with all her fury; and in that moment she seized her kitchen shears and stabbed deep into the Beast's most vulnerable spot of all.

Her baby screamed.

The monster screamed.

Claws came clawing toward her.

But Stella had crawled inside the slash of wound she had made in the monster's ball sac, and the Beast couldn't find her. From inside his ball sac she stabbed the Beast over and over again until black blood covered her and she was gagging from the noxious effluvial waste products flowing from his guts.

About a million years passed.

The Beast staggered. He hiccoughed.

He fell.

Stella felt herself falling. She was going to die after all.

The Beast crashed to the ground.

Stella discovered she was alive, and her baby was alive, because the monster's liquidy sac had protected her from the fall just as her own womb had saved her baby.

She felt the thrumming vibration of the Beast's heartbeat as it quivered and grew fainter. And then it was over.

The Beast was dead.

NOW YOU'VE DONE IT, the baby said. I WAS SUPPOSED TO BE THE SECOND EVIL COMING AND NOW YOU'VE RUINED MY CHANCES

"Oh, baby," Stella said.

She felt nothing but love for the little thing, who couldn't know how pointless it was to worship a noxious orange Beast, who was, to top it off, dead.

"Come on out now, baby," Stella said. "Be born. And after you're born I want you to forget all this nonsense. The Beast is dead. You don't need to fulfill the Biblical prophecy any longer. There's no need for you to be anything more in this world than a baby, just a little baby, and there is no need for me to be anyone except your mother and I'm going to love you a whole lot."

A mighty contraction came and the baby slipped out.

Stella cut the cord with her kitchen shears.

She began to nurse her baby for the first time.

"You were right, baby," she said. "Those kitchen shears did come in handy."

Stella felt a little sad when the baby didn't answer. Instead of the typical sarcastic remark, which was exactly the kind of thing Stella would have expected from her baby in situations like this one, her baby just lay there nursing. Stella could tell by the dreamy unfocus of her baby's eyes that all the demon energy had gone right out of her little one. In the tradition of all babies everywhere this baby remembered nothing of what had come before. It acted like any baby would, spitting up a little green stuff before it recovered and began to nurse again.

Stella looked into her baby's eyes and felt how wonderful it was to be a mother. She wanted the moment to last forever.

But it was getting a little uncomfortable sitting there inside the dead Beast's ball sac as they nursed together with black blood all over them not to mention the afterbirth and other viscera.

So Stella crawled out.

Chaeropus ecaudatus

Chapter Thirty-Six
The End of the World

The first person Stella saw after she crawled out of the dead Beast's ball sac with a baby in her arms was Mary Mbwembwe, who came bounding toward her and rubbed against her legs exactly as if she were a big cat, and Stella remembered that cats always land on their feet.

In her teeth Mary Mbwembwe was holding Stella's L.L. Bean tote bag, and in it was the house cat from Bibi's house, a cat the panther loved with as much tender care as if it were her very own child.

Next to greet Stella was the black chow known as Margie Peach.

"You're alive, you're alive!" Margie Peach yipped, and licked the baby's face clean.

Margie Peach's pack was all there, too, and they barked joyously, and then they cried along with the baby, both for joy at their victory and with sadness for the friends they had lost in battle.

The goat with seagull feathers in her pelt loped over and with gentle eyes and gestures made it known that she wanted to hold Stella's baby, so Stella handed the baby to the goat, and the goat took the child and brought it to the edge of the waters, and bathed it, and carried it to a nearby shipping container, after which the goat brought the baby back, cleaned and swaddled.

They were still too sad and scarred from the battle at first to notice the changes in the air and the earth all around them. The Beast's carcass and the bodies of the fallen were beginning in at first imperceptible ways to renew themselves, like a spring flood renews the earth and causes fresh things to grow. The contours of the Beast's body had already begun to soften. A tinge of green freshness was growing up from the ground and it began to cover the dead, and before too long, a miracle, a soft and mossy hill stood where once the body of a terrible thing had lain. And they would name the hill Venus Mons. And wild growing things began to spread out from the pit, at first just a border of fresh life at the edge of its mouth, but then widening, green and pink and rippling, with flowers and vines and grasses growing up through their toes and paws and hooves; and this carpet of new life kept on growing and spreading out in every direction, in a rush of green and floral-berry colors as far as they could see.

"Behold the Earth, made new again," Margie Peach said gratefully.

"The President was the Beast of Revelation," the Doberman said dreamily. She was overcome to think that her theology had become the literal truth and that she no longer needed to rely on faith alone.

The baby began to cry, just like a normal baby would under the circumstances.

The dogs bowed heir heads.

The goat and panther and California Condor sang their prayers.

All across the world the living things began to seed themselves into the ground and to mingle and to flourish, in exactly the way the good earth had flourished, long ago, before God had cast out the Beast, and before the Beast had settled down on the Earth and spoiled it. And it seemed to Stella as if all that had come to pass in her journey from Barstow to Nethalem had become in an instant the old story, which was now at an end.

Here she was at the beginning of a new story.

In the beginning there was an abundance of Green.

The Sky was new and fresh.

Plants sprang up and grew over all the ugly places.

Sunlight fell upon the face of the earth.

A Panther stood by a young Mother's side.

A Dog led her Pack.

There was also a Condor.

And a Bear with her child.

And a Goat and a Crow, who were soon to be lovers, because in this brave new world no one would ever think twice about such things.

There was a host of other earthly creatures, singing.

There was a Baby with a poopy bottom.

"Well that was something," Stella said.

Book Seven

Beginnings

"Carrying the little meth babies under each arm, like footballs."

Chapter Thirty-Seven
Parthenogenesis, Perhaps

Much to everyone's relief the world started turning and the sun began to come up again every morning as usual. They hadn't been sure of those things, given recent events. Every day more gentle creatures found their way to Nethalem, and joined their community. The grass-loving species soon stopped being scared that the meat-eaters would eat them. The meat-eating species stopped being surprised by their lack of interest in eating meat. Now and then they would grab a fish for a meal but such urges were rare and quickly died out as the days passed, and they discovered far more pleasure in watching the fish frolic and multiply, there in the waters of the bay. Only the Doberman did not enjoy being near the water. She could not help remembering that there were not one, but two Beasts in the book of Revelation, one coming from the Earth, and the other out of the Sea, and she did not want to tempt fate.

Not long after, Stella's dearest friend Bibi came over a hill carrying the two little meth babies under each arm, like footballs, and in that moment when she first saw her Beloved, Stella would know for sure that she had made the right choice to break up with Lix Tetrax for good by stabbing him in the balls rather than letting him have his way with her.

They discovered one day, almost accidentally, that each and every one of them was female. The entire planet had gone double-X. There must surely have been some male critters around at some point on that final day when they battled the Beast, they thought. But none of them could remember any, and if there had been any men, it seemed they had later decided to run off one by one into the wild.

The she-beasts worried at first that they might be destined to be the last of their kind. But the kindly Margie Peach told them about her experience raising whip-tail lizards, an all-female species that did just fine without any men whatsoever. They listened to her story of the whip-tail lizards with hope and joy, and they took heart from her teachings. Because of Margie Peach they had renewed faith that, after putting them through all this trouble, Mother Earth wasn't going to let them down now.

The Doberman remained the most theological among them. She concluded from the evidence that Man alone had been saved. She doubted that any females at all had been taken into Heaven. It occurred to the Doberman for the first time to question the ways that followers of her old faith had trafficked openly in the deprecation of her sex. But she forgave them, and she forgave God, too, in the end. After all it was Adam who was made in the image of the Creator, not Eve, and God could not be held accountable for His prejudices, especially when His prejudices came from ignorance and not malice.

They remained there in Nethalem. It felt like home. The pit from which the Beast had risen had renewed itself and had become a cornucopia of delights and it was impossible for them to imagine leaving it. Over the walls of the pit, which so recently had been burned black from the passage of the Beast, there now grew a rich carpet of deep pink flowers that sent up a sensuous fragrance, and the formerly jagged edge of the pit had smoothed into soft and fragrant lips, so that anyone who came near the opening would be filled with a sense of wonder and well-being. And they named the opening *poontanga'a'* for the way it attracted all lovers of nectar. The birds would fly into it as far as they could, exploring, but no matter how far they flew they never reached the bottom, and they came back blissful, with reports of soft pink floral terraces growing and flowing down as far as they ever could fly, and at some point they always became so intoxicated with rapture from the fragrance that they would forget their quest and fly back out again.

Margie Peach and the Doberman became fast friends in spite of their philosophical differences. Almost every day they would debate whether recent events were caused by a mysterious chemical agent, and could thus be scientifically explained, or if these events reflected the will of God himself. They would paw over Stella's little pink pocket Bible, and Father Juan del Rosario's giant golden Bible, and they would study the collection of science magazines Margie Peach had assembled in her travels, which to Margie Peach were precious relics of the before-time, because they were were full of fragmented but useful scientific reports of those last desperate days.

"You have to admit, the main elements of our experience were foretold in the Holy Writ," the Doberman would insist. "The Plague. The Comet. The Beast. The Baby."

"But the ending is different," Margie Peach would say. "So I admit nothing."

And they would nip and growl and then go off to dig holes.

The Welsh Corgi and the beagle were inseparable. In the last battle they had both sunk their teeth into the Beast's Achilles heel together, and they had hung on together, too, all the way until the very end. Secretly they both believed that their attack on the Beast's Achilles heel, with all its mythological significance, had been the true cause of the Beast's downfall.

The chocolate-colored lab got to work teaching all of the non-dog animals the art of esophageal speech, a skill that had, for some reason, come easily to dogs alone. She used the teaching method that she had once used to teach patients how to speak after laryngeal surgery, a way of belching out words from the digestive system, rather than vibrating the voice box via the respiratory system. Wolves and coyotes were the quickest learners, followed by the big cats, then birds, then pigs, then ruminants and bears and other animals, a progression that tracked closely with the chocolate-colored lab's predictions based on each animal's internal physiology and which had nothing to do with their relative intelligence. All of the animals caught on quickly, with the exception of the *genus felis*; house cats alone seemed disinterested in the exercises and they never practiced and they never mastered it.

At first the chocolate-colored lab had fretted and scratched with worry about whether she would ever be able to teach esophageal speech to those whose native language as humans had been Arabic or Spanish or Vietnamese or Chinese or Malayalam or French, or Swahili. The doctor worried that her own dependence on English would condemn these people to a pidgin tongue—to a second-class way of speaking—and that this difference in speaking, in turn, might eventually lead the non-native English speakers to be treated as second-class citizens, simply because of their accents or their lack of grammatical correctness. But one morning the veil lifted: the doctor realized she wasn't teaching laryngeal vocal techniques in English at all. No: from the very first, the whoosh and growl and coo of their new animal anatomies had altered their formerly human way of speaking, so that by now they were all communicating in a brand new language, one that was rich and animal and common to them all. The truth of it—that all of them had somehow effortlessly learned to communicate in the same melodious language of barks, growls, tweets and resonant wheezes—renewed the doctor's wonder at the resilience of living things.

About the same time that the doctor discovered that they had developed a language all their own, Margie Peach and the Doberman discovered that they could no longer read. One day the orthographic markings on the pages of Stella's little pink pocket Bible and Father Juan del Rosario's giant golden Bible looked like complete jibber-jabber. It happened instantly. There was no warning. At first they were grief-stricken. Soon the loss seemed less important. They consoled one another and then they ran off to dig. Many years later they would create a wholly new orthography, appropriate to their wholly new language, and they would write their own new stories in their own new way of writing. And the first story that Margie Peach and the Doberman would write together would be the story of the Night of the Yellow Puff-Ball Mushroom Cloud—the night when the world changed forever, and for the better. Together the two dogs wrote the book you now hold in your very own two mitts.

Not everything was perfect in the years to come. Stella's baby, named Pashupati, grew up to be a reckless child who would eventually leave Nethalem to seek out the Beast, whom Pashupati believed was still alive and gathering strength in the Yellowstone Caldera, until the time came for the actual, for-real Final Battle, after which the Beast would reign on Earth forevermore. Pashupati never came back. Stella would carry this sadness for the rest of her life, in just the way so many mothers carry the sadness of children who turn away from their mothers and become strangers, harboring open contempt for the very women who bore them and loved them.

As for Stella, she would live another nine hundred and thirty years, and Bibi nine hundred and thirty-one, and the former meth babies, named Yajuj and Majuj, twelve thousand years apiece; and Mary Mbwembwe and the rest of them for even longer than that, so long that most of the original warriors in the Battle of the Beast are all still alive, and they are helping Margie Peach and the Doberman recall the details of this story accurately, and they have seen their children's-children's-children's-children-times-a-thousand-thousand-and-then-some-children flourish on this earth, each generation living longer than the last.

But that part of the story is still to come. Just now we're at the part where all is right in the world, and where three babies play on the green soft grass while their mothers hug and kiss and watch their children with loving care. Josefina Guzman and her lover, the Crow, are splashing in the bay, playing a game something like water polo with Wanda Lubiejewski and her daughter and the dogs; and Major Eureka Yamanaka has just caught a thermal current up into the sky, and she is flying very high, and she is gazing out over the vast clean Pacific to the West; and although Major Eureka Yamanaka can't make out the words her friends are saying on the ground far below, she can hear their laughter as it floats up, and she can see from the way they hold their heads high as they work and live and play together that all will be gloriously well.

So it is written.

Woof Say All!

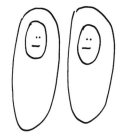

Author's Note

The Book of Dog is the story of heroic and world-saving deeds done by small creatures, working together, and it is told by literal bitches.

I have always believed that when people work together they can change the world, no matter how insignificant or powerless they might feel on their own. It was with that idea in mind that I wrote this book.

I'd love to hear from you. You can reach me through my website, at:

larkbenobi.com.

Thank you for reading The Book of Dog.

~ Lark Benobi

ecopistes
migratorius

Acknowledgments

Thank you David Tristram. You come first.

Thank you Dad. The pigeon on the facing page is for you and so is the marbles game I drew on the second-to-last picture in my story.

Thank you Mom. This is mostly a story about motherhood and its many trials and it would be so much fun to share it with you.

Thank you Ellen Zensen, Nancy Unger, Carol Peters, Anne Oshetsky, and Bob Oshetsky for being enthusiastic early readers.

Thank you Mrs. Patterson for teaching me how to read. Thank you Mrs. Gilles for teaching me how to read Aeschylus. Thank you Goodreads pals. Thank you, writers of books, and readers of books. Thank you Everybody. You are my constant inspiration.

Thank you Jason and Paul. Knowing you changes my life for the better every day.

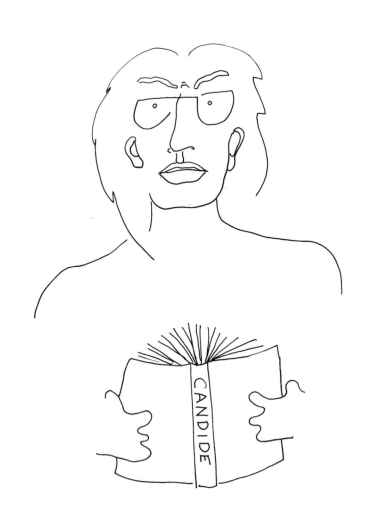

About the Author

Lark Benobi is a playful pen name for Claire Tristram, who is a sometimes-serious writer.

Claire Tristram is also the author of the novel *After* (Farrar Straus & Giroux). Her short stories have appeared in Fiction International, Hayden's Ferry Review, Alaska Quarterly, North American Review, and many anthologies. She has contributed to the New York Times, the Chicago Tribune, Wired, Fast Company, Salon, and many other magazines, and she is a three-time Article of the Year recipient from the American Society of Journalists and Authors. She lives in Santa Cruz, California, with her beloved family.

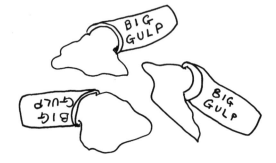

Printed in Great Britain
by Amazon